Susannah
✦ and the ✦
Purple Mongoose
Mystery

Susannah
→ and the ←
Purple Mongoose
Mystery

by **Patricia Elmore**
illustrated by **Bob Marstall**

SCHOLASTIC INC.
New York   Toronto   London   Auckland   Sydney

Text copyright © 1992 by Patricia Elmore.
Illustrations copyright © 1992 by Bob Marstall.
All rights reserved. Published by Scholastic Inc., 555 Broadway, New York, NY 10012, by arrangement with Dutton Children's Books, a division of Penguin Books USA Inc.
Designed by Joseph Rutt.
Printed in the U.S.A.
ISBN 0-590-48465-6

2 3 4 5 6 7 8 9 10   40   6 7 8 9/9 0/0

To my mother,
Winona Harper Elmore

*Kind and sensitive lady, you taught
me to love books, encouraged me to write,
and made the hard time beautiful.*

*Special thanks to my editorial adviser,
Judith Serin, for her invaluable help.
Thanks, also, to Helane Zeiger and
my critique group, especially
Charlene Weir.*

→ Chapter 1 ←

The first fire happened before Susannah Higgins and I entered the case. We didn't even know about it that June afternoon when we skateboarded to Quiggy's house.

Quiggy — her name was really Miss Quigley — was a friend of Susannah's grandmother. I'd been to her house before with Susannah. It was an old brown house with a spiky iron fence around the front yard.

That June day, when Quiggy called to say she had a surprise, I went along again. It was something to do, at least. So far, I'd spent my summer vacation helping Susannah practice for the Black Poetry Recitation contest. And it didn't look like life was going to get any more exciting. Not only did our detective agency have no cases to solve, but Pop had just in-

1

formed me that he couldn't afford to send me to camp with Susannah in July.

It was a cool, foggy afternoon, as usual in summer here near the San Francisco Bay. I skateboarded at half speed because Susannah was still getting the hang of it. Even so, she kept yelling, "Slow down, Lucy!"

Her face grim behind her glasses, Susannah teetered along with her arms flailing and her ponytails bouncing. I slowed down. After all, the smartest sixth grader in Oakland, California, can't be good at everything, can she?

I jumped my skateboard onto Quiggy's walk and raked my stringy blond hair out of my eyes to look at the tall, narrow old house. It was second from the corner, next to a smaller house. On the other side of Quiggy's house was a row of boarded-up stores that had gone out of business months ago.

Toby's truck wasn't there. Too bad. I'd kind of hoped Quiggy's good-looking nephew might have dropped by to do some repairs for her, as he did sometimes.

Susannah careened past me into the driveway by the abandoned stores and stopped. "Lucy, look!" she gasped.

I picked up my skateboard and ran to see. At the end of the driveway, where Quiggy's garage used to be, was a pile of blackened rubble.

"Oh, there you are, girls!" Quiggy trotted down the driveway, her face wrinkled in smiles. Wisps of gray hair sprouted from under her battered straw gardening hat.

"What happened to your garage?" Susannah asked.

"Burned down last week." Quiggy's mouth tightened, making lines around it like the spokes of a wheel. "Well, let's not talk about that. Come meet — "

"But how did it happen?" Susannah peered over her glasses, which had slipped to the end of her nose.

Quiggy shrugged. "The fire department thinks somebody might have set the fire deliberately."

Susannah's brown eyes widened. "It was arson?"

"But who would do a thing like that?" I said. I couldn't imagine anybody wanting to hurt Quiggy.

"Some nut, I guess." Quiggy shook her head. "Let's drop the subject. I've talked to the fire department, the police, and the insurance company till I'm sick of it. Now I want you to meet somebody. Theresa!" she called.

A thin dark-haired girl slouched from be-

3

hind the house, her hands in the pockets of stiff new jeans. She was smaller than Susannah or me but about our age. Her pink T-shirt was still creased from the package. Her narrow eyes glanced at us warily.

"Theresa, dear," Quiggy said, "this is Susannah Higgins and her friend Lucy. They'll be in the sixth grade with you next year, so I thought you'd like to meet them."

Theresa didn't answer or even smile. She turned her eyes to a lizard slithering down the side of the house.

That's when I got the strange feeling I'd seen her somewhere before.

"Theresa's my new foster daughter," said Quiggy.

"What?" I wasn't expecting that.

"I *knew* you'd be surprised." Quiggy put her arm around Theresa. "I'm just afraid she's going to be lonely living here with an old woman like me, and with Ruth."

Ruth, Quiggy's younger cousin, was at least forty. She'd lived with Quiggy for years and acted like the house was hers. Ruth always seemed irritated when Susannah and I came to visit and kept telling us not to touch things. Maybe she was jealous that Quiggy had visitors. Or maybe she just didn't like kids.

4

"I like it here," Theresa said.

"Bless your heart." Quiggy hugged her. "Now you girls get acquainted while I clean up and fix some refreshments. I know you're going to be great friends." She hurried down the driveway and around the back of the house.

We stood silent. Adults always want you to be friends with kids you're not sure you even like. I couldn't imagine ever being friends with this angry-looking girl. But I wished I could remember where I'd seen her before.

Susannah spoke first. "You really lucked out on your foster mother. Quiggy's great."

Theresa shrugged. "She's okay. But Ruth hates me. She says I make noise and have bad manners. She won't even let me pet her dog."

"Ruth doesn't let anybody touch Pipsqueak, except Quiggy," I said. "Don't mind her. Ruth doesn't like anybody but Pipsqueak and Quiggy."

I followed Susannah down the driveway. Hands on hips, she looked at the ashes and burned wood.

"Lucy, this is serious," she said. "The fire could have spread to the house if the fire trucks hadn't arrived in time. Who could have done it?"

I glanced at her. "Think we can find out?"

"We'll sure try. Theresa? Where were you when it happened?"

"In bed," Theresa said. "Quiggy woke me when she smelled smoke."

"Did you see anything before that?" Susannah asked.

"I told you — I was asleep," Theresa said irritably. "Anyway, I can't see the backyard from my room in the attic."

Susannah walked into the backyard, looking at the scorched bushes as if hunting for clues. A dog began barking behind a high fence that separated the next yard. Pipsqueak's shrill yips answered from a window above. Susannah looked up at it.

"That's Ruth's room, isn't it?" she asked. "Didn't she hear anything that night?"

Theresa shook her head. "She sure slept soundly for somebody who claims my radio keeps her awake."

"I bet the fire was scary," I said.

"You should have seen it!" Theresa's face came alive. "Flames were shooting out of the garage roof, then the door blew away. We had to stay in the front yard, but I could see down the driveway. There were fire fighters all over the place."

I could imagine it. I'd seen a fire a few years

ago, when a second-grade kid tried to burn down a shed used to store playground equipment.

"Any idea who did it?" Susannah looked at Theresa. "Did Quiggy say anything to you?"

"No." Theresa turned toward a ball hanging from the big tree near the fence. "Want to play with my new tetherball?"

"Won't Ruth complain?" asked Susannah. "We're right under her window."

"She's gone shopping," said Theresa. "We can make all the noise we want."

As we approached the tree, the dog next door barked more furiously — a big, mean dog from the sound of him. Quiggy's neighbor must have gotten him since the last time we were here. I was sure glad the high board fence was between us.

"Shut up, Rowdy — you know me!" Theresa yelled at the fence. But the dog next door kept yowling, and Pipsqueak answered from Ruth's room. "It's you two he's barking at," Theresa said, as if it were our fault.

Tetherball's about the only sport Susannah's good at. Theresa was, too. The way she bashed the ball, teeth clenched, I was glad this wasn't a boxing match.

Watching her, I suddenly knew where I'd seen that face before.

"Stop that!" yelled a harsh voice. "What the blazes is going on?"

We froze, then looked around. Nobody was there.

"Shut up that noise!"

The voice came from the other side of the high fence.

Quiggy hurried out to the back porch. "Really, Mr. Reid!" she called. "Children have a right to play."

"Tell them to play in the park then!" the invisible voice yelled back. "I'm trying to take my nap."

"Oh, come now, Mr. Reid!" Quiggy looked exasperated. "It was your dog making all the racket."

"My dog?" Mr. Reid sounded indignant. "What about that yappy thing your cousin calls a dog? At least Rowdy only barks at strangers. He's a good watchdog."

"Huh!" Quiggy snorted. "Then how come he didn't bark when somebody set fire to my garage?"

Susannah and I looked at each other. The excited sparkle in her brown eyes told me she'd found a new mystery. I almost hated to tell her I'd already solved it.

→ Chapter 2 ←

"You're sure it's the same girl?" Susannah squirmed into her denim jacket as we headed back to her place, carrying our skateboards. The late afternoon had turned chillier as the fog rolled in.

"Sure I'm sure. You'd remember her, too, if you'd been in second grade with me." Susannah had gone to a different school then.

I'd never forget: the fire alarm ringing, smoke pouring out of the shed across the playground, fire trucks screaming through the gate, and then the principal hauling a girl from another second-grade class away from where we were lined up. I could still see her twisted, angry face.

"It was Theresa all right," I said. "They caught her red-handed."

"And you never saw her again?"

"I told you. They said she'd moved away."

"Huh," Susannah grunted. "Sure is suspicious, her turning up at Quiggy's right before the fire."

"Right," I said. "She's obviously one of those whatchamacallits that go around setting fires."

"Pyromaniac, you mean?" Susannah is a walking dictionary. "Maybe, but we need proof." Being a judge's granddaughter, she's big on proof.

Me, I'm big on action. "Are we just going to wait around till Theresa burns Quiggy's house down?"

"No, but we're going to find out more about Theresa and where she's been all these years. First thing tomorrow."

But the next morning I had to clean the kitchen. Pop's been fussier about housekeeping since he started dating Mae Jones. Susannah's grandmother had things for her to do at home, too, so it was late afternoon by the time we headed for Quiggy's.

"First we'll find out where Theresa used to live," said Susannah. "Then we'll check there and find out if she ever set any fires."

A fire truck passed, siren wailing, then another one. They turned into Quiggy's street a block ahead. We started running.

By the time we arrived, the fire trucks were blocking the street, and people had gathered to watch. Smoke poured over the roof of Quiggy's old house.

"Is anybody inside?" Susannah grabbed the nearest arm in the crowd. The man didn't know.

"Please," Susannah cried out, "does anybody know if Quiggy and — "

"It's all right, dear." A plump white-haired woman turned to us. "I saw them all drive off — even the dog — long before I spotted smoke from the back porch and called the fire department. I live in the house behind, you see."

I started breathing again and watched the fire fighters racing with hoses to the back of the house. Knievel Jones would have loved it. Not that I wished he were here. He was usually our partner, but so far we were doing fine solving this case without him. Thank goodness, because when it comes to things I can do without, Knievel is right up there with stewed prunes and broiled liver. To make matters worse, his mom just happens to be the lady Pop dates.

A middle-aged man stood near us. "I told Miss Quigley the old wiring in this place was a fire hazard and needed replacing," he growled in a voice I recognized. Mr. Reid in person was bald, except for a fringe of gray hair. With his bushy eyebrows and turned-down mouth, he looked as grumpy as he'd sounded across the fence yesterday. He wasn't much taller than me and not exactly fat, but he looked flabby under his wrinkled shirt.

Just then Quiggy's old car swerved up behind the fire trucks, and she sprang out. Ruth followed, clutching Pipsqueak.

"Where is she?" Quiggy demanded. "Where is Theresa?"

"Wasn't she with you?" asked the white-haired woman.

"No! I sent her back home! I've got to . . ." Quiggy started for the house.

"No, Quig!" Setting down Pipsqueak, Ruth all but tackled Quiggy. Quiggy struggled to get away, but Ruth was taller and stronger.

A fire fighter came from the backyard, wiping his face on his sleeve. "This your house, ma'am? Afraid I have bad news."

"Oh, no!" Quiggy gasped.

"Yes, ma'am. Your back porch is a total loss."

"My foster daughter . . ." Quiggy pulled away from Ruth. "She may be trapped in her room in the attic."

"No, ma'am," the fire fighter said. "Nobody's in the house. We checked every room."

"Thank heaven," Quiggy sighed. "But then where *is* she?"

Susannah and I glanced at each other.

"Ma'am" — another fire fighter came up — "did you have newspapers stacked on the porch?"

"No, why?"

"Because the rubble is full of paper ash — lots of it. I'd say somebody set fire to a pile of newspapers on your porch."

A murmur rippled through the crowd.

"Impossible," said Quiggy. "We store the old newspapers in the hall, by the basement stairs, to take to the recycling center."

"Well, they're not there now," the fire fighter said.

"I don't understand," said Quiggy. "Who could have put them on the porch?"

"Theresa knew where they were." Ruth's voice was shrill. "I knew when you took her in there'd be trouble."

Everybody around us grew quiet, and people started drifting away.

"Are you suggesting Theresa set the fire?" Quiggy's gray eyebrows knotted in a tight frown.

"Of course she did!" Ruth's mouth trembled with fury. "You heard her say she'd get even when you sent her home before the movie for using bad language."

Quiggy shook her head. "We all say things we don't mean. And you did provoke Theresa into calling you names in the car. Sometimes I think you're jealous of the poor child."

"Jealous! Of that . . . that nasty little . . . ?" Ruth sputtered. "Oh, Quiggy, how can you stand it? She eats like a pig, uses gutter language, turns the TV on so loud I'm going deaf — and you hardly even scold her. We were so happy till she came, and now — "

"She's had a hard life, Ruth. And her manners are improving."

"Some improvement!" Ruth scoffed. "Your precious foster daughter just tried to burn the house down. Face the facts, Quig. There weren't any newspapers on the porch when we left. Now all of our newspapers are gone from the hall. Nobody could have gotten in the porch door, because I bolted it myself. And who but our dear little Theresa had a key to the front door?"

"Theresa would never — oh!" Quiggy stopped suddenly.

Theresa was coming up the walk.

Quiggy ran to hug her. "Where on earth have you been, child?"

"In the park." Theresa looked bewildered. "What happened?"

Quite an actress, that Theresa, I thought.

⇢ Chapter 3 ⇠

"You're right, Lucy," Susannah agreed as we walked home. "We can't wait till we get more evidence. Two fires since Theresa moved in — that can't be a coincidence. We've got to warn Quiggy."

We waited until late the next morning, when Ruth would be at work. She had a half-day job as a bookkeeper. We didn't want her hanging around while we told Quiggy what we knew.

Nobody answered the front doorbell, so we walked around back, passing blackened rosebushes as we crunched over the scorched grass and waded through piles of ashes. Mr. Reid's dog started barking next door and set Pipsqueak yipping upstairs.

The porch was gone. There was nothing but

17

rubble. The back of the house was scorched black and a sheet of fresh plywood covered the doorway to the kitchen.

Susannah squatted to examine something in the rubble. "Look at this, Lucy."

But I was more interested in the new red truck coming down the driveway into the backyard. I wished I'd brushed my hair. Or better yet, that I were older and prettier. Toby, Quiggy's nephew, always made me feel that way.

He was the best-looking guy I'd ever seen this side of a TV screen. He worked as a handyman. Quiggy always called him when she needed a sink unstopped or worn steps replaced.

Toby stepped down from the truck, grinning at us. "Hi, girls. Long time no see. Love that T-shirt, Blondie."

He meant the screaming-green T-shirt I'd just bought at a yard sale. Knievel Jones said it made me look like a gangrened frog. But Toby had my kind of taste. I decided I didn't even mind his calling me Blondie.

"Looking for Aunt Quiggy and Theresa?" Toby hauled an unpainted door from the back of the truck. "I dropped them off to buy cleaning stuff while I picked up some lumber."

He looked at his watch. "I've got to get back soon and pick them up. Want to ride in the back?"

"No thanks," said Susannah before I could say yes. "Look, Toby." She brushed away ashes from a blackened board. A bolt held it to another strip of wood. "It's the porch-door latch. Ruth was right. It *was* locked from the inside."

Toby whistled. "That sure proves whoever set the fire didn't get in through the back porch. And come to think of it, the person must have come through the house, because he — or she — picked up the newspapers stacked in the hall."

Susannah straightened and looked toward a second door, over by the driveway. Three steps led down to it. "Is that the basement door?"

"Yes, but it stays locked, and so far as I know, Quiggy has the only key now. She gave me one a while back because I've got stuff stored down there, but I lost mine." Toby climbed into his truck and started the motor. "So the only way I can see anybody getting into the house is through the front door. I guess Ruth and Theresa have keys to that, but I sure don't."

That cinched the case against Theresa, I thought as Toby backed the truck out.

"Theresa has to be crazy," I said. "You don't burn a house down just because you can't go to a movie."

Susannah walked over to the basement door and tried the knob. It was locked. The dusty windows looked locked, too. We strolled down the driveway. There weren't any basement windows on that side, and the windows on the first floor had iron grilles on them.

I followed Susannah around the front and along the side by Mr. Reid's fence to the backyard again.

"See," I said, "the front door's the only way to get in."

"Looks like it." She thought a minute. "Let's go talk to that lady who called the fire department."

At the end of the backyard was a low hedge. On the other side I saw a larger yard and the back of a faded pink stucco house. We'd reached the hedge when I heard a crunching noise behind us.

A man was coming up Quiggy's driveway. Turning the corner of the house, he halted before the pile of rubble. He stood there, hands in pockets, as if hating to soil his blue

suit by walking through the mess. He lit a cigarette and shuffled. Finally he jerked his pants
legs up and waded in.

He pushed back the board covering the
kitchen doorway. He was stepping through
when we came up silently behind him.

"Looking for someone?" Susannah asked.

He spun around, startled. "I . . . uh . . . is
Miss Quigley home?" He was slim, with sparse
black hair brushed back from a sunburned
face.

"No," said Susannah. "Can we give her a
message when she gets back?"

He hesitated. "Well, say George Peterson
came by. Tell her I'll come back later."

"Can I tell her what you wanted?"

"She'll know. Especially after what's happened. Tell her I'm prepared to make her an
offer she can't refuse."

With that Mr. Peterson waded back through
the rubble and headed down the driveway.

I stared at Susannah. "An offer she can't refuse! Sounds like the Mafia."

"But an offer for what?" Susannah frowned
over her glasses. "And strange, he didn't seem
surprised there'd been a fire here."

We crossed the backyard to the hedge. The
yard on the other side stretched all the way to

21

the corner behind Mr. Reid's house. The white-haired woman was weeding a bed of pansies. She glanced up at us from under her blue cloth hat.

"Hello. You must be friends of Theresa." She looked at us more closely through her sunglasses. "Oh, I saw you girls at that awful fire yesterday. Poor Quiggy, what a terrible thing."

"Really." Susannah introduced us, and the woman said she was Mrs. Weinberger. "You called the fire department, didn't you?" Susannah asked.

"Yes." Mrs. Weinberger joined us at the hedge. "Luckily, I'm always gardening about then, so I saw the smoke right away. Good thing, or the house might have burned down."

"If anybody had come into Quiggy's yard before the fire, would you have noticed?"

"I'm sure I would have."

"And you were here the whole time Quiggy was gone?"

"Except when I went inside to answer the doorbell. Somebody had sent me roses." She smiled in a puzzled sort of way. "Beautiful roses, and I still don't know who sent them or why."

"You don't?" Susannah's eyebrows shot up.

"No idea. The card said 'From a secret admirer.' " She smiled shyly. "Maybe that man I met at the senior center."

Susannah frowned. "How long were you in the house?"

"A few minutes. The delivery boy insisted on singing 'You Are My Sunshine' for me. Then I had to find a vase and cut the stems so the roses would last and . . ." Mrs. Weinberger looked troubled. "Oh, dear, do you think that while I was in the house somebody set that fire?"

"Could be. Do you remember what florist brought the flowers?"

"I'm afraid not." Mrs. Weinberger rubbed her trowel against her chin thoughtfully. "Wait a minute, I do recall a name. I'm not sure where I saw it. Of all strange things, Mongoose. Funny name for a florist."

"What did the delivery boy look like?"

"Oh, about eighteen, I'd say. Blond. Wore a sleeveless purple T-shirt. His bicycle was purple, too. Must be his favorite color. Had a tattoo on one arm."

"What kind of tattoo?"

"A bird with webbed feet. A loon, I think. I

saw one on a TV nature program the other night." She looked at Susannah with interest. "Why do you want to know?"

"Just curious," she said. But after Mrs. Weinberger went back to her weeding, Susannah was thoughtful.

"Interesting. Maybe Theresa's not our only suspect. What if somebody sent those roses to get Mrs. Weinberger out of her yard? So she wouldn't see the person sneak through Quiggy's backyard and set the fire."

"Maybe Theresa sent the roses," I argued. But that didn't seem likely. Roses were awfully expensive. And anyway, Theresa didn't need to sneak through the backyard; she had a key to the front door. "Or what about that Mr. Peterson? He wants something from Quiggy — maybe badly enough to burn down the house."

"There's only one way to find out. Come on, Lucy, let's go back to my place fast."

"Aren't we going to wait for Quiggy, to tell her about Theresa?" I protested.

"Not yet. It sounds like there might be another suspect. Let's find out who sent those roses."

Back at Susannah's grandparents' house, we looked in the phone book for the Mongoose Florist. There wasn't one.

→ Chapter 4 ←

Susannah wasn't surprised.

"The name's too weird for a florist," she said. "A video store or a toy shop I'd believe, but not a florist. Mrs. Weinberger probably read it wrong."

So we sprawled on her bed, eating tuna sandwiches, and looked up florists with names that began with M. Susannah had her own telephone line, as a private detective should. Her grandparents had agreed to it, as long as she paid her own phone bills.

Susannah dialed while I stared at the snake pictures decorating her walls. She calls herself an amateur herpetologist and dreams of having a snake of her own. But her grandmother says she can just keep dreaming.

She called the Monguio Florist first and asked, "Do you have a delivery boy with a purple bicycle and a loon on his arm?"

Leaning close to the receiver, I heard a voice answer: "Look, kid, I haven't got time for jokes." *Click!*

"Try another approach," I suggested, "like not mentioning the loon tattoo right away."

"Good point," she agreed.

Next she called the Montrose Flower Shop and, in a grown-up voice, asked for their delivery boy with the purple bicycle.

"Lady, how should I know what kind of bicycle he's got? I'll have him phone you when he gets back with the delivery van, if you want."

"Never mind, thanks." Susannah slapped her head as she hung up. "What idiots we are! Florists don't deliver flowers on bicycles. They use vans. Obviously, that guy with the purple bicycle wasn't from a florist."

"Then we'll never find him."

Susannah thought a minute. "Maybe he works for a messenger service — one of those places businesses use to deliver packages."

I'd seen messengers like that weaving their bicycles through the traffic in downtown Oakland. I opened the yellow pages again and looked up messenger services. "There isn't any Mongoose," I said.

But there were some that began with M, so Susannah dialed them. She asked if they'd delivered roses to a Mrs. Weinberger on Norris Street yesterday. They all said they never delivered flowers to anybody, only letters and packages.

"So" — Susannah hung up and drummed her fingers on the phone table — "he doesn't work for a messenger service either. Our only clue is the name Mrs. Weinberger saw — Mongoose."

"Funny she'd mix up a name like that," I said. "I wonder where she saw it, anyway. On his shirt? On his bike, maybe? Or — "

"On the bike? Hey, wait a minute." Susannah sat up straight. "Maybe Mongoose is a kind of bike."

"Could be," I said. "Somebody who knows about bikes could tell us." I hated saying that, because if anybody knew about bikes, it was Knievel Jones.

"Right." Susannah picked up the phone and dialed. "It's time we brought our partner in on this case, anyway."

A moment later I heard Knievel screeching over the phone as Susannah held the receiver away to protect her ears.

"Mongoose?" he yelped. "You kidding? That's one of the best all-terrain bikes there is. They cost hundreds — some of them over a thousand."

"Thanks, Jones," Susannah said. "Then you'd better get over here right away. We need your help."

We were waiting downstairs when Knievel arrived. Through the living-room window I saw his bike leap the walk and heard the tires squeal as he braked. He paused to rake back his mop of red hair, then wiped the fender and gave it a loving pat. It's just a secondhand ten-speed, but Knievel likes to pretend it's a real motorcycle.

"This better be a good case." He cocked his head importantly as Susannah opened the door. "I'm missing baseball practice."

"Don't let us keep you," I urged hopefully. "It's probably going to be real boring."

I'll never know why Susannah took him into our detective business. Knievel may not be the worst kid in Oakland, but he sure tries.

Knievel unzipped the windbreaker he thinks

of as a real leather jacket while Susannah explained about the roses.

"Wait a minute," I interrupted. "You forgot to tell him about Theresa. Remember when that shed burned down on the playground back in second grade, Knievel?"

"I sure do. Some of the kids tried to blame me."

I recalled that Knievel had had a perfect alibi: He was sitting in the principal's office, as usual.

"Well, the girl who did it is Quiggy's foster daughter."

"No kidding!" Knievel whistled. Then he frowned. "Funny, I saw her a couple of months ago. When we were playing that basketball team from Alameda. She was with the family of that jerk-face who kicked me while I was shooting."

"The guy you had a fight with after the game?" I remembered him. A hulk with big teeth.

"Yeah. I'd have flattened him, only his folks dragged him away. And that girl went with them."

"What's his name?" Susannah demanded.

"Arthur," said Knievel. "Arthur something."

"It's a funny kind of last name." I'd noticed

the guy's name at the time but couldn't quite recall it now. "Something hard that ought to be soft."

"An oxymoron?" Susannah asked.

"You said it," Knievel agreed. "Arthur's an ox and a moron, all right."

"His name, you ignoramus," I said. "An oxymoron's two opposite things."

"I know that," Knievel lied. "Yeah, it was some name like . . . like Pillowrock. But not exactly."

"Pillow*stone?*" Susannah suggested.

"Stone. Yeah," I said. "But something else soft."

"Comforter? Cloud? Feather?" Susannah looked at us hopefully. "Fur? Breeze?"

"Feather," Knievel echoed. "That's it. Featherstone. Arthur Featherstone was his name."

I could have killed Knievel for beating me to it.

◈ Chapter 5 ◈

The phone book listed an Arthur J. Featherstone. Trusting he was the father of our old basketball buddy, we set out for the address, on the other side of Oakland.

It took two buses and a walk down four blocks. The neighborhood wasn't fancy but not run-down. About like where I live: apartment buildings and small houses with mowed lawns. Except for the Featherstones' house, where the weeds were past mowing.

A little kid answered our knock. His T-shirt came down to his knees and looked like it hadn't been washed since its former owner threw it away.

"We're selling raffle tickets for the Recreation Fund," Susannah announced, flourishing the batch she'd gotten from her grandmother, who's always raising money for good causes.

The door would have slammed except that Knievel's foot was in the way. He does have his uses.

"Say" — I mustered up a friendly tone — "it says Featherstone on the mailbox. This isn't where Arthur Featherstone lives, is it?"

The door opened again. "Who wants to know?" A husky boy with big teeth shoved the little kid aside.

"Hey, man, good to see you." Knievel managed to sound as if Arthur Featherstone were his long-lost friend.

I don't know if Arthur remembered us, but he acted as if he did. He probably needed all the friends he could get.

"What's this scam with the raffle tickets?" he asked. "Any money in it?"

"Not for us," Knievel said. "By the way, where's that girl I used to see you with? Theresa, I think her name was."

"Oh, her." Arthur snorted. "She used to live with us, but she's gone now, and good riddance. Mom threw her out when she tried to burn the house down."

. . .

Susannah and I left Knievel at the bus stop and went straight to Quiggy's. We had to tell her what we'd learned about Theresa right away.

Quiggy wasn't home, but Theresa was. Maybe our faces told her this wasn't just a friendly visit.

"What do you want with Quiggy?" she demanded.

Susannah looked at her a minute, then seemed to make up her mind.

"All right, I'll tell you. We think you set fire to the porch."

"*What?*" she screeched. "That's a lie!"

"Oh, sure." I rolled my eyes. "And it's a lie that you set a fire at the Featherstones', right?"

Theresa took a step backward. "How did you . . . ?"

"Theresa," Susannah said gently, "you need to talk to a psychologist who'll help you stop wanting to set fires."

"*I didn't set any fires!*" Theresa shrieked. "If you think anybody's going to believe your lies — "

"Come off it," I said. "Arthur Featherstone told us the whole story of how you tried to burn down their house."

"I didn't!" Theresa breathed hard. "They always blamed me for everything. I'm the one who ran to tell the neighbors to call the fire department."

"Got scared, huh?" I said. "Look, Arthur said they left you home when they went out for pizza, and you were so mad you set the kitchen curtains on fire."

"No." Theresa shook her head. "The grease caught fire while I was frying a hamburger, and — "

"Quiggy's garage wasn't any accident," Susannah said.

"Garage?" Theresa looked startled. "I was asleep."

"Sure you were," I said. "Just like you were playing in the park when the porch caught fire."

"I *was*."

I snorted. "Next you'll say you didn't set fire to the playground shed back in second grade."

Theresa swallowed. "The sh-shed?"

"Don't say you weren't there," I said. "I saw you."

To my surprise, Theresa burst into tears.

"Oh, what's the use?" She flopped into a

chair and hid her face in her hands. "Nobody ever believes me."

Susannah hunkered down beside her. "We might, if you try telling the truth."

Theresa jerked away.

"I — I didn't. . . ." Her voice was thick behind her hands. "I'd never d-do a thing like that to Qu-Quiggy. She's . . . she's the only one who's been nice to me."

Susannah looked at her thoughtfully. "What about the Featherstones? Weren't they nice, too?"

"No! I wish they were dead. I mean . . ." Theresa looked up at us, as if frightened at what she'd said. "I told you, it was an accident. Please" — she looked at Susannah desperately — "you've got to believe me."

Susannah studied her face. "And the shed that caught fire back in second grade, that was an accident, too?"

"Yes. I mean . . ." Theresa met Susannah's eyes, then looked down at her hands. "That was a long time ago."

I glanced at Susannah triumphantly.

"I didn't mean to burn the shed down." Theresa took a shuddering breath. "I was only trying to burn my report card and a letter from

the teacher to my first foster parents. But"
— she sighed — "all it got me was the Featherstones."

I couldn't help feeling sorry for her. But
setting Quiggy's house on fire, that I couldn't
forgive.

"Please" — Theresa fixed her eyes on Susannah — "please don't tell Quiggy about the
shed. She likes me."

Susannah gazed at Theresa over her glasses
for several moments. "*Did* you set fire to
Quiggy's porch, or the garage?"

"No, I swear."

Susannah nodded. "I think I believe you. At
least you deserve the benefit of the doubt."

I was beginning to have a doubt myself.

Theresa gave Susannah a grateful look. "I
swear I didn't do it. Honest."

"But if you didn't," I said, "who did?"

"I wonder," said Susannah, "if that Mr. Peterson had anything to do with it. Maybe the
boy on the purple Mongoose knows."

✦ Chapter 6 ✦

"Are there many Mongoose bicycles around, Jones?" Susannah asked the next morning after we'd told Knievel about our talk with Theresa.

"Not a lot of purple Mongooses, I bet," said Knievel. "At least, I've never seen one."

"Good. Then maybe we can find it. That's your job, Jones."

"And just how do I do that?"

"Start by checking bicycle shops. Find out if anybody's seen one lately."

So while Knievel made the rounds of bicycle shops, Susannah and I headed back to Quiggy's.

"We've got to find out some things," she said as we walked. "First, who is Mr. Peterson and what is the offer he says Quiggy can't refuse? Oh, darn!" She snapped her fingers. "We

38

forgot to tell Quiggy he came." Susannah hates forgetting things.

"No big deal. We'll tell her now. What else do we want to find out?"

"How the arsonist got in."

"Through the front door," I said. "How else?"

"But Toby says only Theresa and Ruth have keys to the front door, and Quiggy, of course. Anyway, if I were going to set a fire, I sure wouldn't use the front door, because anybody could see me from the street. I'd slip around back, where I'd only have to worry about Mrs. Weinberger seeing me. And I'd be clever enough to send her flowers to get her out of her garden at exactly the right time."

"Pretty neat," I admitted. "There's just one problem with your theory. The porch door was latched from the inside, and Toby says Quiggy has the only key to the basement. So how would you get in the house from the backyard?"

"That," said Susannah, "is the puzzle."

As we turned down the driveway into Quiggy's backyard, I heard hammering. Yanking Susannah back, I borrowed her comb to rake out my hair.

Toby was putting up the skeleton of a new

porch. He already had the new back door in place and a cement block to substitute for the old steps. I smiled at him as I giant-stepped up to the door — and into a bucket.

Nothing wrecks your style like wedging your foot in a bucket. I tugged at my shoe, my face burning, while Toby howled with laughter. He laughed so hard that Quiggy peered out of the kitchen.

"It's not funny, Toby," she scolded as Susannah extricated my foot. "The poor child could have hurt herself."

"Sorry. She knows I didn't mean it. Right, honey?" He rumpled my hair, looking so apologetic that I decided I didn't mind. "Forgive me, Aunt Quig?" He blew her a kiss.

"Don't waste your charm on me. Just finish the porch."

I was surprised at her grumpiness. Usually Toby made her laugh. She must have been tired from scrubbing soot off the kitchen cabinets.

"Theresa went for groceries," she told us as she washed out a blackened sponge at the sink. "You can help me while you wait for her, but keep out of Toby's way. I want that porch finished before he takes off for Jamaica or China or wherever it is this time." She shot him a reproving look. "Wish I could afford all that travel. Not to mention a new truck."

Toby winked at her. "I've made some good investments, Aunt Quig." He went back to hammering.

Susannah picked up a sponge and started scrubbing a cabinet. "Quiggy, a Mr. Peterson came yesterday while we were waiting for you. Said he'd come back today. He wanted to make you some kind of offer."

"That man!" Quiggy groaned. "Why won't he leave me alone?"

"What does he want?" I asked.

"Something he can't have," Quiggy said firmly. "I don't want to discuss it. And please don't say anything to Theresa — or especially Ruth. She gets so upset over every little thing. Oh, here's Theresa. Will you girls have lunch with us? Mrs. Weinberger brought me some nice soup."

"Thanks, we'd love to," Susannah said.

"Ruth's late, so we won't wait for her. Toby," she called, "care to join us for soup and sandwiches?"

"No thanks, Aunt Quig." Toby leaned around the door. "I'm leaving soon. Got business to attend to."

"Business?" Quiggy snorted. "A horse race, I'll bet."

"Now, Aunt Quig." Toby hastily changed the subject. "I keep forgetting to ask, did you find the keys I left here last week?"

"No. Sure you left them here?"

"I must have. No big deal. I've got spares for the other keys but not for the one to your basement." Toby went back to hammering.

We ate in the big dining room, with its row of old plates displayed on the rack high up on the oak-paneled wall. There was more fancy china in the glass-doored cabinet and a clock with a brass pendulum that no longer kept time. The room gave me a cozy feeling.

"This house must be really old," I said to Quiggy as I slurped my soup.

"My grandfather built it," Quiggy said proudly. "It needs some repairs, but it's a good solid house."

Susannah gazed into space. I knew she was dying to ask Quiggy about Mr. Peterson but couldn't with Theresa there.

Theresa was telling Quiggy about a run-in she'd had with Mr. Reid next door.

"He yelled at me because I cut across his front yard."

Quiggy sighed. "He's been so irritable ever since he lost his job. He's really good-hearted under all that gruffness, but lately . . . well, I guess he's worried about money, poor man. Just avoid him, honey."

The phone rang in the hall. Quiggy wiped her lips and went to answer it. She came back looking worried.

"Your caseworker is coming," she said to Theresa.

Theresa froze. "What does she want?"

"She didn't say." Quiggy started clearing the table. "I'm afraid she's heard about the fires and thinks this isn't a safe place for you to live. Go change your clothes. And I'll have to ask you girls to leave."

We sure hadn't learned much, I thought as Susannah and I left. We still didn't know what Mr. Peterson wanted, much less whether the arsonist could have gotten in through the basement.

"Where're you going?" I asked Susannah. To get to her house, we should have turned right past Mr. Reid's house on the corner. But Susannah went left, toward the boarded-up stores next to Quiggy's driveway.

She halted in front of them, frowning. "Used to be a beauty parlor and a laundry and a little grocery store here. Now they're closed."

"So? Stores close all the time."

"But all three? And why hasn't the owner rented them to somebody else?" She walked up to the beauty parlor and studied the sign: NO TRESPASSING. LEVIATHAN CORP.

"Maybe nobody wants them," I said. "Or maybe this Lev . . . Levia . . ." I gave up trying to say the name. "Maybe they're going to tear these down and build something better."

"Let's see what else is on this block." Susannah continued walking, turning left again at the corner and around to the street behind Quiggy's house, where Mrs. Weinberger lived.

There wasn't much to see — just a few houses with drawn shades and overgrown yards, as if nobody lived there, and a building like a warehouse that looked abandoned, too.

"Looks like the only houses with people in them are Quiggy's, Mr. Reid's, and Mrs. Weinberger's," said Susannah.

"Yeah," I said. "So what?"

"I don't know, but it's interesting."

We went back the way we'd come. We'd almost reached the buildings by Quiggy's when I saw somebody watching us from the other side of the old beauty parlor. It was Quiggy's cousin Ruth.

"Hmm." Susannah's brown eyes met mine.

"Why's Ruth so interested in what we're up to?"

"Probably thinks we're stealing Quiggy from her," I said.

As we came closer, Ruth turned and hurried up the walk to Quiggy's house. The front door slammed behind her.

→ **Chapter 7** ←

We found Knievel sprawled on Susannah's doorstep, picking at a hole in his jeans.

"About time," he grouched. "I've been waiting an hour." Knowing Knievel, that meant fifteen minutes.

"What did you find out?" Susannah demanded.

Knievel leaned against the door, looking smug. "Well, I went to Mike's Bikes and started looking at twenty-one-speeds like I was going to buy —"

"Never mind the details," I interrupted. "Did they know the guy with the purple Mongoose?"

"No, so I went to the next place. They had some really neat racing bikes, so I got to talking with the guy about —"

"Get to the point," I groaned.

"I'm just telling you how I got information."

"*What* information?" I pleaded. "Did they know him there?"

"No, so I went to — "

"Jones," Susannah begged, "could you skip to the part where you learned something?"

He looked hurt. "Well, it was the fourth place, and the lady there knew all about racing tires. Like she told me the best kind for — "

"Susannah," I sighed, "if I murder him, will they give me a life sentence?"

"I'll give you a medal," she said. "Jones, did the lady know the guy with the purple Mongoose?"

"I'm getting to that. See, I told her the bike I really want is a Mongoose, and she said I had good taste." Knievel paused to be sure we got that. "They had lots of models, but I told her I wanted purple. She said a guy bought the last purple Mongoose last week. A really expensive one, she said."

"A guy with a loon tattoo?"

"Yeah. She mentioned it herself. I didn't even have to ask."

"What's his name?"

"Harry. She doesn't know his last name."

"Did she know where he lives?"

"Kind of." He paused importantly.

"Kind of?" I echoed. "Get to the point, Knievel, or I'll start a rumor you sleep in a bunny suit."

Knievel thought that over. "Well, she said he came in a bus with a couple of other guys. An old school bus painted blue with a big rainbow across it. He told her they live in it."

"Well, that's some help," said Susannah, "but not much. Finding the bus won't be any easier than finding the Mongoose."

"Wrong," said Knievel. "She's seen that bus a couple of times before, parked down by the Bay. She told me where."

Susannah slapped his shoulder. "Great work, Jones. You're terrific."

"Yeah," he agreed.

It took a good hour's biking to find the place. But sure enough, parked on a dirt path well back from the water was an old bus painted blue with a huge rainbow across it. Not a very good rainbow. The colors weren't even in the right order. I could have done a better job.

Nobody was around, and we couldn't tell if anybody was in the bus.

"Listen," said Susannah, "we've got to play

this right. Remember, our story is that Knievel's looking for a Mongoose and heard Harry has one to sell.''

"Don't I wish.'' Knievel looked wistfully down at his old ten-speed.

"Well, act like it's true,'' Susannah said. "And let me do the talking. Above all, don't mention the fire or that we suspect — oh, no!'' She stared past us in horror.

The rainbow bus was driving away.

I leaped on my bike. "Wait!'' I yelled. "Come back!''

Knievel's bike shot past me. A moment later he rode beside the bus, banging his fist on the door.

The bus stopped as I got there, Susannah right behind me. The long-haired driver turned down his blaring radio and stared out at us. He looked about twenty, as did the man next to him, who had a mass of black braids.

"What do you want, kids?''

"Are you Harry?'' asked Susannah.

"Nope. He left a while ago on that fancy bike of his. Decided not to go down to Santa Barbara with us. Said he'd rather go look at ducks and geese.''

"A nut case, that Harry.'' The other man laughed. "All he cares about are bicycles and birds. He'll bore you to death talking about ducks."

Susannah looked bleak. "Didn't he say where he was heading?"

The driver shrugged. "Said something about wanting to see those geese they got up in Canada. Well, we got to go. It's a long ride to Santa Barbara. Have a nice day, kids." He shifted gears, and the rainbow bus whined and coughed toward the freeway.

"Darn!" Susannah slapped her thigh. "If we'd just gotten here earlier."

We started home in glum silence. But as we came to a McDonald's, Knievel braked.

"I'm starved," he announced.

For once, I agreed with him. "Come on, Susannah. Let's stop for a hamburger. And a root beer, if you can lend me the money." As usual, my wallet had more jingle than crinkle.

We were chaining our bikes to the rack when I saw Harry.

It had to be him. I could make out what looked like a tattoo on his arm as he got on his purple bicycle.

"Harry!" I yelled. "Wait!"

But he sped away. And even Knievel couldn't catch up with the purple Mongoose.

⇝ Chapter 8 ⇜

"Grunch!" That's Susannah's own made-up cussword, the only one her grandmother allows. "Well, at least we know he's still somewhere around. We'd be out of luck if he'd gone to Canada, like that guy thought he might."

"But how are we ever going to find him?" I asked.

Susannah stamped her foot. "If we only knew where he was going!"

"Did you notice the gnarly wheels on that Mongoose?" Knievel looked smug. "You don't buy a bike like that just to ride around the corner."

"So where *do* you ride it?" Susannah asked.

"Mountain trails, anywhere the going's rough."

"Terrific," I said. "So all we have to do is head for the Sierras."

"Sometimes there are races, too. I could find out if there are any around here soon. And, hey, why don't I stake out that McDonald's, in case Harry goes back there? Of course," he added casually, "I'll need money for expenses."

"Thanks, Jones," said Susannah, "but we can't afford your appetite. Find out about races. And go back to the bike shop. Ask the lady to find out how we can reach Harry if he comes back there. Meantime, we'll work on other angles of this case."

Our next move, she said, was to go back to Quiggy's tomorrow. We'd ask Quiggy about Mr. Peterson and also take a look at her basement.

Thanks to Susannah's appointment with the eye doctor, we couldn't make it to Quiggy's till after lunch the next day. By then Knievel had found out that the only mountain-bike race coming up, near San Jose, wasn't until September.

"Grunch!" Susannah groaned. "We can't wait that long. We've got to think of another way to find Harry. Well, for now, let's see what we can find out about Mr. Peterson."

But when we got to Quiggy's, her car was gone. So was Toby's new truck, to my disappointment. A pile of fresh lumber lay near the skeleton of the back porch.

Theresa was scraping blistered paint off the kitchen wall.

"Could we take a look around the basement?" asked Susannah, after introducing Knievel. "It's possible the arsonist got in the house through a window down there. If so, we might find a clue."

"Okay." Theresa laid her scraper on the counter and led the way to the hall.

The door to the basement was behind the stairs. I noticed Quiggy had started a new stack of newspapers there. Theresa opened the door and pulled a string, but the bulb high above the stairs didn't light.

"Must have burned out. It was working when Toby helped me move stuff down from the attic a couple of weeks ago," said Theresa.

"Do you know if anybody's been down here since then?" Susannah asked.

"I don't think so. Quiggy and Ruth are scared of spiders . . . and rats."

I wasn't fond of them myself. "Guess we can't explore the basement," I said hopefully.

"There's no way we can reach that bulb to change it."

That didn't stop Susannah, of course. She sent Theresa to get a flashlight. Then she started down the stairs, raking the beam of light over the railing as she went.

I politely let Knievel go next. I didn't want him dropping a spider down my back.

Susannah stopped on the third step. "Look at this."

I leaned over Knievel's shoulder to inspect the circle of light on the handrail. I could just make out a smudge in the dust.

"Handprint," said Susannah. "Pretty fresh. The dust's hardly settled on it. Don't touch the railing," she added.

She continued slowly down the stairs, searching until she found another smudge near the bottom.

The basement was huge and gloomy and smelled of mold. The cobwebbed ceiling and cement floor stretched all the way under the house, disappearing into darkness behind us. Boxes and discarded furniture were piled all around.

Ahead, a sickly glow seeped in from the backyard through two grimy windows. After inspecting the dust around the frames, Susannah tried to raise one. It didn't budge. Neither did the other.

Susannah moved away, flashing her light onto the stuff piled up all around. The beam paused on a broken rocker and some boxes. "This the stuff you brought down from the attic, Theresa?"

"Yes. How did you know?"

"Simple. No cobwebs on it. What's that?" The flashlight beam rested on some metal shelves draped in cobwebs with a ladder propped alongside.

"That's where Quiggy lets Toby keep his old tools, since there's no room at his condo."

He hasn't used them in several generations of spiders, I thought.

"We've got to see if there's another way into the basement," said Susannah. "Are there any more flashlights, Theresa?"

"I don't think so."

"Could you get some matches then? I saw a couple of boxes by the stove."

When Theresa came back with them, Susannah gave a box to Knievel and a box to me. "Jones, go search for an opening over there." She motioned to the side of the basement by the driveway. "Theresa and I'll take the side by Mr. Reid's house. Lucy, you go that way."

She meant the darkness behind us, toward the front of the house. It wasn't a job I wanted, but I wasn't about to say so in front of Knievel. I took my box of matches and headed bravely off into the shadows beyond the stairs.

Susannah doesn't know how I hate the dark. Since darkness doesn't bother her, I guess she thinks I feel the same way.

The air was dank and chilly. I shivered, wishing I'd brought my jacket. At first, I could see my way by the glow from the windows behind. But when I rounded a pile of boxes, even that dim light disappeared. I struck a match and kept going. The sooner I got it over with, the sooner I could get back.

Things rustled in the darkness. Rats, I thought with a shiver. I lit another match.

Blundering around more boxes, I saw a glimmer far ahead. Another window? But as I moved forward, it vanished. Another pile of boxes was in the way. I struck a match and circled them.

Now I saw the glimmer again. I kept moving, brushing cobwebs aside.

I smelled dirt, and my head banged against the ceiling. Lighting another match, I saw a dirt crawl space ahead, probably under the front porch. Daylight glinted through a low window. I crawled on hands and knees toward it.

Something rustled behind me. Looking around, I saw only darkness. I fumbled for a match and dropped the box as something clammy slid down my back.

I shrieked and clawed at it.

Then I heard an awful sound — Knievel's giggle.

"You scum!" I shook his rubber spider out of my shirt and punched at him. He dodged expertly.

Suddenly Knievel noticed the light ahead. "Susannah!" he yelled. "I've found another window!"

"*You* found?" I squawked.

Susannah's flashlight bounced through the darkness. The beam dipped as she stooped to enter the crawl space, Theresa behind her. I scurried ahead of them, shoving Knievel aside to get to the opening.

It was a small screened rectangle at ground level, about a ruler's length high and two rulers wide. It looked out into a thick bush, through which I could see Mr. Reid's fence.

"Hmm." Susannah poked all around the frame. One side gave way and swung out, squeaking. "Pretty small opening."

"I could get through it," Knievel bragged.

"Any skinny kid could," I retorted. I couldn't help glancing suspiciously at Theresa.

"A skinny grown-up could, too," she said quickly.

"Shhh!" Susannah grabbed my arm.

I heard footsteps crunch outside. Banging heads with Knievel, I pressed my face to the screened window and saw feet. Two feet in black men's shoes standing on the other side of the bush.

The feet went on tiptoe. Their owner must be peering into the living room. Then they moved away, crunching toward the backyard.

Susannah scrambled back the way we'd come, flicking on her flashlight. I scurried behind her, crouching so as not to hit the low ceiling of the crawl space. We had to get to the back windows and see what he was up to.

Skirting piles of boxes, I finally reached the windows and hunched down with Susannah by the one nearest the back door. Outside, I saw a man in black shoes and gray trousers near the pile of lumber. A skinny man with a sun-burned face and black hair.

Mr. Peterson was looking at the skeleton of the new porch. He jingled his pockets and shuffled, paying no attention to Rowdy's barking next door and Pipsqueak's yipping upstairs. Checking his watch, he took a box of matches from his pocket.

Susannah sprang to open the door to the backyard, but it didn't budge.

"Theresa," she whispered desperately, "how do you unlock it?"

"I don't know." Theresa looked scared.

Through the grimy window I saw Mr. Peterson strike a match.

⇥ Chapter 9 ⇤

"We've got to get out of here!" I gasped. "He's burning down the house!"

I twisted the doorknob and pushed, but the door wouldn't open. Knievel shoved me aside and banged it.

"Turn the dead bolt," Susannah said urgently.

I elbowed around Knievel and twisted the knob that worked the bolt, then opened the door.

The sudden brightness made me squint as I stumbled up the three steps to the backyard.

Mr. Peterson gaped at us. Then he turned as Quiggy's car came up the driveway. Shaking out the match, he hurried to meet her.

"Good, I was hoping to catch you home." Mr. Peterson shoved the matchbox in his pock-

et and turned on a smile as Quiggy climbed out of her car.

Quiggy looked at him without enthusiasm. "Now look, young man, I've told you time and again — "

"I know, I know." Mr. Peterson shuffled his feet. "But wait till you hear my new offer. You can't turn this one down."

"Oh, but I can." Quiggy took a bag of groceries from the backseat. "Now good day to you, sir."

"But . . . but, Miss Quigley!"

"Good day," she repeated, sweeping past him. "My house is not for sale, and that's that."

Mr. Peterson glared at her back. His red, peeling face had a nasty look. "You'll be sorry, old lady," he muttered, then headed down the driveway toward the street.

Theresa ran to Quiggy. "That man," she gasped, "tried to set the lumber pile on fire."

"What?" Quiggy stared at her. "Are you serious?"

"Looked like it," said Susannah. "Unless he meant to light a cigarette but forgot to put one in his mouth first."

"Oh, sure," Knievel scoffed. "We saw him — "

"Theresa can tell you," Susannah said quickly. "Sorry, Quiggy, we've got to go now." She hurried down the driveway.

Knievel and I glanced at each other but didn't argue. We followed her to the front corner of the house where the spiky iron fence began. Susannah motioned us behind a jasmine bush.

Mr. Peterson was opening the door of a yellow Datsun parked across the street. He paused, glanced at his watch, closed the door, and crossed the street again. This time he headed up Mr. Reid's walk.

We slipped through an opening in the iron fence and crept along the front of Quiggy's house, keeping behind the geraniums. When we'd gotten as close to Mr. Reid's house as we dared, we crouched, watching.

Mr. Peterson jabbed Mr. Reid's doorbell, looked at his watch, and jingled his pockets. Rowdy barked furiously in the backyard. Mr. Peterson checked his watch again, shuffling his feet. He obviously didn't know it was Mr. Reid's nap time.

Then I heard Mr. Reid shout, "Shut up, Rowdy!" and the door opened. I waited for him to yell at Mr. Peterson for waking him up, but he didn't. He let Mr. Peterson in, and the door closed.

"Interesting," Susannah said softly.

"Yeah," I said. "So old Reid's mixed up in this."

"I'll sneak under his window and try to hear what they're saying." Knievel began squirming through the geraniums.

"No." Susannah pulled him back. "Too risky. We might blow our cover." She meant our cover as ordinary, innocent kids. "Too bad we can't follow Peterson when he leaves. The way he kept looking at his watch, he must have an important appointment." She sighed. "But we can't follow his car on foot."

"We should have brought our bikes," I groaned, "or our skateboards."

"Leave it to me." Knievel jumped over the iron fence and took off running.

"That scuzz-brain," I said. "Thinks he can get back with his bike in time."

For once I'd underestimated our partner. Knievel raced across the street and opened the door of the yellow Datsun. Then he darted around to the hood and lifted it.

"Ooo, that's bad," said Susannah.

"Real bad," I agreed. "And it'll be worse if he doesn't hurry before somebody sees him."

I caught my breath as Mr. Reid's door opened and Mr. Peterson came out. They shook hands as the hood slammed down. By the time Mr. Peterson crossed the street, Knievel was strolling away down the block, whistling.

"Let's hope Jones knew what he was doing," Susannah whispered as Mr. Peterson got into the Datsun.

A moment later he jumped out, scratched his head, and lifted the hood. I guess he didn't know much about cars — after staring at the engine, he slammed the hood and tried to start the car again. Then he got out and banged his fist on the hood. I thought he'd throw a tantrum, but he just blew on his fist. Then, looking at his watch, he locked the car and hurried on foot down the street.

Susannah and I let him get half a block ahead, then followed. Mr. Peterson led us several blocks to a busy street lined with shops. Suddenly he halted and looked around. We ducked into an alley, and when we cautiously peered out, Mr. Peterson was gone.

"Looking for somebody?" said a voice behind me.

Whirling around, I saw Knievel Jones.

"You louse!" I snarled.

He smirked. "Is that nice after all I've done? What would you do without me?"

"Interesting thought," I said. "I dream about it all the time. What did you do to Peterson's car?"

"Nothing much. Just took the cables out of the distributor cap. All he had to do was put them back."

Susannah tugged my arm. "There's a BART entrance down the street. I bet that's where Mr. Peterson's gone."

BART is the subway for San Francisco and Oakland and some other places. We raced into the station, then quickly braked. Mr. Peterson was at the ticket machine, fumbling in his pocket.

Luckily, we had our student tickets with us, and we reached the turnstile seconds after Mr. Peterson passed through it. When we got down to the tracks, he was pacing the platform and, of course, jingling his pockets. We waited at the far end behind a pillar.

"At least now we know what he wants from Quiggy," Knievel said while we waited for the train. "To buy her house."

"But why?" Susannah frowned. "Why is he so desperate to buy a run-down old house? It's not even in a good location, with those abandoned stores next door. And, if he wants the house so badly, why was he about to burn it down?"

"It doesn't make sense," I agreed.

When the train came, Mr. Peterson got on. We crowded into the next car and stayed close to the door. At each stop, we looked out to see if he was getting off. When he did, in downtown Oakland, we followed.

We let Mr. Peterson get a block ahead as we galloped down Broadway. At Seventeenth Street he turned the corner and went into a building.

"Hurry," said Susannah. "We've got to find out who he's going to see in there."

→ Chapter 10 ←

We pushed through the revolving door Mr. Peterson had entered and paused in a vast marble lobby. The shiny black floors reflected blurs of people hurrying to and from the elevators. I didn't see Mr. Peterson anywhere.

"We've lost him," I groaned.

Susannah looked around. "There must be a list of the companies here somewhere. Oh, there it is." We followed her to the black signboard with white letters posted by the elevators.

I scanned the list — mostly doctors and dentists — but nobody named Peterson was there.

"We've got to find him." Knievel made karate chops in the air. "I can't wait to start sweating that guy."

Susannah sighed. "This isn't TV, Jones. I just want to find out . . ."

That's when I saw trouble coming. Big trouble. More than six hefty feet of it in a uniform and with a gun in a holster.

He stalked close enough for me to hear his raspy breathing and read SECURITY on his badge. There was no love for kids on his fat red face.

He towered over us, hands on hips. "Why are you kids here?" he bellowed.

"Well, uh . . ."

"Uh, well, uh . . . ," Knievel added unhelpfully.

Then, like a miracle, I saw the very person I always dreamed would come to my rescue when I needed him most. Toby was getting off an elevator. I ran to him and grabbed his arm.

"Toby," I whispered, "act like we're with you, okay?"

But Toby didn't seem glad to see me. In fact, he scowled. "Look, kid, this is no time for games. Just had a tooth pulled, and I feel rotten." Jerking his arm from my grasp, he went out the revolving door.

I was crushed. It felt almost as bad as having my own tooth pulled.

The security guard grabbed my sleeve.

"Out." He clamped a hand on Susannah's shoulder. "All of you."

She stared at him wide-eyed. "But I've got an appointment with . . . er . . . Dr. Nakamura on the seventh floor."

"Me too," I said quickly.

"And me," said Knievel.

"Yeah?" The guard eyed Knievel. "When's *your* baby due?"

"Huh?"

"Dr. Nakamura is an obstetrician," said the guard. "She delivers babies."

"Oh," said Susannah. "We . . . uh . . ."

"Out!" barked the guard. He shoved us toward the revolving door.

"But we have to . . ." Susannah looked at me desperately.

I tried to dig my heels into the slick floor. "Hey, who do you think you're pushing?" I grabbed a marble pillar.

Knievel dug in, too. "Get your paws off me," he said, clinging to the other side of the pillar.

The guard looked from one to the other of us, his face redder than ever. "Just wait'll I—"

Knievel stuck out his tongue, and the guard

lunged for him. That was my chance. I ran.

Susannah was already sprinting for the elevators. I dived into one with her and jabbed the button marked CLOSE DOOR. As the doors came together, Knievel raced up. I owed him for letting me get away from the guard, so I held back the doors.

Knievel squeezed in as they closed, almost on the guard's nose. Susannah pushed a button, and we went up.

"Whew!" I slumped back, glad we had the elevator all to ourselves.

"Yeah," said Knievel. "Hey, where are we going?"

"The tenth floor," said Susannah.

"Why?" I asked.

"A crazy hunch. One of the companies listed downstairs is a real-estate developer, the one that bought those buildings next to Quiggy's."

"You think Peterson works for them?"

Before she could answer, the elevator opened on the tenth floor and I saw the sign: LEVIATHAN CORPORATION. REAL-ESTATE DEVELOPMENT.

⇸ Chapter 11 ⇽

"We'd like to see Mr. Peterson, please," Susannah said in her most grown-up voice.

The receptionist at Leviathan Corporation stared at us. Her red fingernails were so long I wondered how she could press the phone buttons in front of her.

"Peterson? Sorry, nobody by that name here."

"He's thin, with black hair, and he's got a sunburn," I said, in case Peterson wasn't his real name.

"Sorry."

"Strange," said Susannah. "Maybe he just came to visit somebody. Wasn't he here a few minutes ago?"

"Oh," said the receptionist. "Come to think of it . . ." She glanced at a slip of paper.

"That's right, there *was* a Mr. Peterson here looking for the boss. Said he was a real-estate agent. You just missed him."

"Very interesting," Susannah muttered when we were back in the hall. "So Mr. Peterson is a real-estate agent. I should have guessed. But why would a real-estate agent want to burn a house down?"

"Too bad we missed him," Knievel grumbled. "I sure wanted to sweat the guy."

"Yeah?" I said. "Since you're feeling so macho, suppose you take on that security guard downstairs. He'll be waiting when we get off the elevator."

"I hate to spoil your fun," said Susannah, "but we're going straight down to the street this way." She opened a door marked STAIRS.

"What do you think Peterson was doing here?" I asked as we galloped down the ten flights, our footsteps echoing in the stairwell.

"I don't know," said Susannah, "but I'm sure Leviathan has something to do with this case."

I opened the door to the street. People were hurrying past and lining up at the bus stop. Cars inched along, horns honking. Now and then a bicycle zigzagged past, weaving freely among the cars.

"Look!" Knievel yelled suddenly. "There he is!"

Careening through the traffic was a purple bike and the boy we'd seen at McDonald's.

"Harry!" we all screeched. "Wait!"

But the purple bike disappeared around the corner.

"Grunch!" Susannah slapped her thigh. "Lost him again. Oh, well," she added more cheerfully, "at least we know he's still around. Surely we can find — "

"Oh, no!" Knievel gawked at his watch. "It's nearly five. Mom'll ground me if I'm late for dinner again."

Pop wasn't going to be pleased with me, either.

"Run!" said Susannah. "We can't get grounded. We've got too much to do."

We hurtled past the stream of briefcases bobbing toward the BART entrance. We were halfway down the stairs when Susannah grabbed my arm.

At the foot of the stairs stood Mr. Peterson, talking to somebody whose back was to us. Then the person turned, and I saw her face.

It was Ruth. She looked even more annoyed than usual.

We turned and sprinted back upstairs, diving through the mass of people hurrying down.

"Think they saw us?" I gasped when we reached the street.

"I hope not," said Susannah. "Take a quick look, Jones."

Knievel ran to peek down the stairs and motioned to us. "They're heading for the turnstile."

"Come on." Susannah hurried toward the stairs. "Stay out of sight, but don't lose them."

We reached the platform in time to see Ruth and Mr. Peterson push their way into a packed train. A huge group pressed behind them. The situation called for desperate measures.

Knievel used his elbows. Susannah used her brain.

"Please," she begged, "we're with that lady who just got on."

I took the hint. "Mom!" I shrieked. "Wait for us!"

People turned to stare.

"Let those poor kids get on the train with their mother," said a woman.

"Let them on!" a man ordered, and the crowd parted to let us through.

We squeezed into the car next to the one Ruth and Mr. Peterson were in. Then we were bouncing along, me smashed between Knievel and a forest of briefcases. A woman reached over to pat my cheek.

"Don't worry, honey, your mother'll be there when you get off at your stop."

"I sure hope so." I tried to squeeze out a tear.

Susannah rolled her eyes.

At the stop near Quiggy's, Ruth and Mr. Peterson got off. We followed and saw Mr. Peterson go to a phone booth while Ruth hurried out to the street.

"Who do we follow?" I said, looking at Susannah.

"Both." She sent Knievel after Ruth while we stuck with Mr. Peterson. When he got off the phone, we followed him back to Quiggy's street, where he paced and jingled his pockets by his car.

Knievel joined us. "Ruth went straight home," he said.

"Bet he's waiting for her to come out," I said.

I was wrong. A yellow emergency truck pulled up, and the mechanic looked under the hood of the Datsun. It took him less than a minute to fix things. Then Mr. Peterson started the car and drove off.

I looked at Susannah. "So Ruth's in this deal with Peterson. I never thought she'd betray Quiggy."

"Me either." Susannah looked troubled. "I thought she adored Quiggy and that's why she lives with her. But maybe the real reason is Ruth can't afford a place of her own."

"Well, she can if Peterson pays her to get Quiggy to sell the house," said Knievel. "Or to help him burn it down."

"But which is it?" I asked Susannah. "Does he want to buy the house or burn it down?"

Susannah stared at the sidewalk. "Maybe it doesn't matter. Maybe it isn't really the house they're after. I have an idea we'll check out tomorrow."

Suddenly Susannah fixed her gaze on Quiggy's house. Turning, I caught a glimpse of a face peering around a shade. Ruth was watching us.

→ Chapter 12 ←

"Aw, give me a break," Knievel moaned the next morning when we got off the bus at the big building on Fourteenth Street. You might say Knievel has an allergy to libraries. "I thought we were going to do detective work."

"We are." Susannah led us upstairs to the Periodicals Room and asked for the index to the *Oakland Tribune*. We parked ourselves at a table with a row of what looked like computer terminals while she flipped through the hefty volume, scribbling numbers on a scrap of paper.

"You've done research before, haven't you, Jones?"

"Sure." Knievel's idea of research is copying a few paragraphs out of the encyclopedia when a report is due.

"Good," said Susannah, "then you can read 'fiche."

Knievel gawked. "Read fish?"

"Microfiche," I said smugly. I'd done research with Susannah before. "It's film of printed stuff. You put it in one of those machines and read it on the screen."

"Oh, sure." Knievel acted like he'd known all along. "Anybody knows that."

I kept an eye on him while Susannah took the list of microfiche she wanted to the librarian. Knievel has a knack for getting kicked out of libraries, but luckily he had a scab on his elbow to keep him busy. He'd picked it good and bloody by the time Susannah brought back a handful of microfiche strips in paper jackets and divided them among us.

I cranked the handle to find the date and page Susannah had jotted down and spotted a headline: *Leviathan Opens New Condos.*

"Susannah!" I whispered around Knievel. "This says Leviathan bought up a row of old houses that burned down and built condos there. That was two years ago."

Susannah came to look. "Interesting. How about you, Jones? Find anything?"

Knievel scowled. "It's in Russian, I think."

Susannah took a look. "You've got the microfiche upside down, Jones."

Once we turned it around, the article told about some office buildings Leviathan Corporation built last April where a row of small stores had burned down earlier.

"Leviathan sure buys a lot of land where buildings have burned down," Susannah muttered.

A shiver shot down my spine. "They already own most of the land on Quiggy's block. She told Peterson she won't sell her house, but if it burned down, she'd have to sell the land."

"For a lot less money without the house," Susannah said grimly. "Not that Leviathan cares, because it's the land they're after, not the house. Come on, you two, we've got to move fast, before it's too late."

As we bounded down the library steps, Knievel said, "But it's Peterson, not Leviathan, who wants to buy Quiggy's house."

"Don't you get it, fuzz-brain?" I said. "Peterson is buying it for Leviathan. Right, Susannah?"

"I think so. If Leviathan plans to tear down the block to put up high rises, they probably want to keep it quiet. There are people who'd try to stop them if they knew, like the Neighborhood Preservation Society. So Leviathan gets an independent real-estate agent, Peterson, to do the buying."

"Yeah, okay," said Knievel. "Only Quiggy won't sell, so they told Peterson to burn her house down."

"Or somebody else," said Susannah. "We don't know for sure Peterson set those fires."

Something bothered me. "If Leviathan's buying up the whole block, what about Mr. Reid's house? And Mrs. Weinberger's?"

"Just what I'm wondering," said Susannah. "Come on, we've got to talk to Quiggy."

We found Quiggy in the backyard, digging up burned rosebushes.

"So that's what's been going on!" she exclaimed when we told her what we'd learned at the library about Leviathan. "I told Sheila Weinberger there had to be some reason this real-estate agent, Peterson, has been so hot for us to sell our houses."

"So Mr. Peterson *does* want to buy Mrs. Weinberger's house," Susannah said. "Mr. Reid's, too?"

Quiggy nodded, and the brim of her ragged

straw hat bobbed down to her nose. "Mr. Reid's ready to sell. Sheila Weinberger hasn't decided yet. But Peterson won't buy their places unless he can buy mine. Reid's driving me crazy to sell."

"But you aren't going to, are you?" Knievel asked.

Quiggy got to her feet, wiping her forehead on her sleeve. "Frankly, I'm thinking about it." Her voice was sad. "It might be best, if I'm up against Leviathan. And it's an awfully big house for just Ruth and Pipsqueak and me."

"What about Theresa?" I asked, startled.

Quiggy sighed. "They're taking her away. In fact, they've already found a family who'll take her next week."

"But why?" asked Susannah.

Quiggy's mouth tightened. "They said she needs a 'firmer hand,' as they put it. They said these other people can handle so-called problem kids better." She snatched off her grubby gardening gloves, looking suddenly angry. "Theresa's moody, I admit, but not a problem. I think Ruth's been telling stories to the social worker."

I wondered if we ought to tell Quiggy what

we knew about Theresa, but I caught Susannah's warning glance. Well, there was something else Quiggy ought to know.

"We saw Ruth talking to Mr. Peterson downtown yesterday," I said.

"Ruth?" Quiggy looked stunned. "No, you must be mistaken. You saw someone else who looks like her."

"No," I began, but Susannah said quickly, "Maybe you're right, Quiggy."

Quiggy gathered up the dead rosebushes. "Well, go see if Theresa's back from the park. I heard some sounds from the attic a while ago, so she must be up in her room. I'm sure she'd love a visit. Poor thing, all this moving around is hard on her."

As we went indoors, Knievel said, "Come on, Susannah, *you* know that was Ruth we saw with Peterson."

"Yes, but there's no point upsetting Quiggy until we can prove Ruth really is involved in the fires."

We'd reached the second floor when I saw Ruth coming down the ladder from the attic.

"Where do you think you're going?" she demanded in her hoarse voice. "You kids roam all over the house like it's yours."

"Quiggy told us to go up to Theresa's room," Susannah said calmly.

Ruth snorted, opened the door to her room and picked up the yipping Pipsqueak, then slammed the door behind her.

We climbed the ladder and knocked on Theresa's door. Susannah waited a minute, then opened it.

This was my favorite room. Quiggy used to let us fool around in there. The slanting wood walls gave me the cozy feeling of being in a tent. There was only one window, opening on the front lawn. The room used to be full of old trunks and cast-off furniture, but all that was gone. Now there was a bed and dresser, a rug and ruffled curtains.

But Theresa wasn't there.

"That's interesting," Susannah muttered. "Then what was Ruth doing up here just now?"

→ Chapter 13 ←

"Well, what's next?" Knievel asked when we'd returned to the backyard. He leaned against the fence. The dog on the other side growled. I was sure glad that fence was between us.

Quiggy was gone and so was her car.

Susannah frowned over her glasses. "We've really got to find Harry. Looks like Leviathan is behind those fires, and Peterson probably set them. But to prove that, we've got to find out if Peterson sent the roses to distract Mrs. Weinberger. And only Harry can tell us that."

"And we let Harry get away — twice." Knievel kicked the fence.

Immediately the dog behind it began barking.

"Now that's interesting," said Susannah.

"That dog didn't bark when we came — just growled. He didn't bark till this minute."

"Yeah, well, he recognizes our smell by now," I explained. "He only barks at strangers."

"Okay," she said. "So why didn't he bark at whoever set the fires? Unless it wasn't a stranger."

I thought that over. "It was somebody he knew. Like Ruth?"

Knievel barked back at the dog — a major mistake. Suddenly the fence slat he was leaning against gave way at the bottom. A huge, hairy black head leered out at us, teeth bared. Knievel pushed the slat back fast.

"Hmm." Squatting, Susannah gently tested the slats around the loose one. The one on the right gave way, too.

"Interesting," she muttered. "With both of these slats pushed out, somebody could squeeze through." She cautiously pulled out the first one partway. A huge snout pushed through, snarling.

I held my breath as Susannah, keeping her hand just out of reach, let him smell it. Then carefully she reached in to pet his muzzle. "Nice dog," she cooed.

The huge red tongue lapped her hand.

She had us pet him, too. I wasn't sure I'd get my hand back, but he just licked it, then gave Knievel's a badly needed washing. Through the open slat, I saw a bushy black tail going like a windshield wiper.

A wicked grin crossed Susannah's face. "If Rowdy just happened to get out . . . well, think we could catch him?"

I got the idea. What better excuse to talk to Mr. Reid than to bring back his runaway dog?

We should have picked a slower mutt. When Susannah pulled the slat all the way back, Rowdy squeezed through and took off like a racehorse.

First he led us around the tree — twice — then dived into the rubble. Knievel and I stumbled out spitting ashes as Rowdy tore down the driveway.

Brakes squealed in the street out front, but there wasn't any blood when I got there.

"There he is!" Knievel yelled. "In that yard across the street. Head him off, Lucy."

Rowdy pawed the dirt, waiting for us to catch up. I felt like a fink, acting like I was coming to pet him while Knievel crept up behind him.

Mr. Reid was waiting at his gate, red-faced

and scowling, when we half dragged, half carried Rowdy home.

"What do you think you're doing, letting my dog out?" he bellowed. "I ought to call the police."

"Sorry, Mr. Reid," Susannah said. "He slipped through a loose slat in your fence. Here, I'll show you."

"Hey, wait, don't . . ." Before he could stop us, we scooted through his gate and into the backyard, Rowdy racing beside us.

I couldn't see why Mr. Reid was so fussy about keeping us out. His backyard sure wasn't much to look at. The weeds hadn't been cut for months, and the few flowers poking out of them looked like mistakes. There was a pile of old bottles and cans near the fence.

"It's along here somewhere." Susannah picked her way through the pile of trash, watching her footing carefully. "Oh, here it is. See, the next one's loose, too." She pushed the boards out from the fence.

Mr. Reid stared at the slats poking out from the fence. "That brat Theresa must have worked them loose. I know her kind, always up to something. Set those fires, too, I bet."

"Lucky the fires didn't spread to your side, Mr. Reid," said Susannah. "You must have been worried."

"You better believe I was," Mr. Reid snapped. "Awful thing, waking up from my nap to find fire trucks next door."

"I guess since you were taking your nap you couldn't hear Rowdy barking," Susannah suggested.

"I certainly did." Mr. Reid sounded indignant. "I woke when he started barking at the sirens."

Susannah pulled a thorn from her jeans. "You didn't notice anybody in Quiggy's yard just before the fire, did you?"

"Certainly not, or I'd have told her."

"Hmm." Susannah peered at him over her glasses. "Any idea why somebody would set fire to Quiggy's house?"

"No. We've never had any trouble in this neighborhood until that brat next door came. Now isn't it about time you kids went home?"

We left. As we walked out to the street, Knievel muttered, "Mr. Reid could've gotten through those loose slats into Quiggy's yard. Maybe *he* set the fire!"

"Yeah," I said. "And he had a motive: If

91

Quiggy's house burned down, Leviathan would buy his."

"Sure, but we need proof," Knievel pointed out.

"Well," said Susannah, "I found something very interesting in his trash pile."

"What?" I demanded.

"An empty lighter-fluid can."

"That proves it," I said. "Mr. Reid set the fire."

"That empty lighter-fluid can isn't proof, but he sure looks like a suspect." Susannah sighed. "We've got to track down Harry and find out who got him to deliver the roses."

That subject was beginning to get on my nerves.

"We better find him soon," said Knievel, "before he heads that Mongoose up to the mountains."

"Or Canada," I said. "Remember, those guys in the rainbow bus thought he might be headed up there — to look at geese, of all stupid things. Must be pretty special geese."

"Mongeese, probably," said Knievel. "Having a Mongoose bike, I bet that's his favorite kind of geese."

I doubled over laughing. "You ignoramus, a

mongoose isn't a goose! It's an animal that eats snakes."

Knievel looked skeptical. "You sure?"

"Sure I'm sure. Aren't I right, Susannah?"

"What?" Susannah looked like she'd just come back from somewhere else.

"Isn't a mongoose a furry little animal, not a bird?"

"Of course. Listen, I've just had a thought." Her voice was excited. "What if Harry's friends were mixed up about his going to Canada to see geese? What if what he really said was he was going to see *Canada geese?*"

"Maybe," I said. "But where would he look for Canada geese?"

"The water-bird refuge at Lake Merritt. It's not far from where we saw him yesterday, and I bet that's where he'd been."

The water-bird refuge is at one end of Lake Merritt, which is right in the middle of downtown Oakland. It was just after nine-thirty the next morning when Susannah, Knievel, and I got there.

We heard the commotion even before we reached it: hundreds, maybe thousands, of birds quacking and honking and squawking.

Dozens of birds cruised on the lake, fluttered in the foggy air, or waddled about the fenced-in feeding area.

Nobody was around except some joggers and a uniformed woman hosing down the feeding area.

"How long do we wait?" Knievel asked.

"Till Harry shows up." Susannah shrugged off her backpack and sat down on the grass. "All day, if necessary."

"What if he doesn't come?" I asked.

"We'll come back tomorrow." Susannah took two books from her backpack: One was a collection of the poems of Langston Hughes, which she was memorizing, and one was called *Snakes as Pets.* I shuddered.

"Shoot," said Knievel. "I thought detective work was supposed to be exciting."

I wandered down to the water with him. One big goose kept chasing the others, trying to be boss. Just like the school yard. This, I thought, was the only lake I'd see this summer. I wished for the hundredth time I could go to camp with Susannah next month.

By eleven, we were ready for lunch. I'd brought leftover pizza for all of us. It was one Pop had ordered, so I dug out the anchovies.

Knievel stuffed his slice into his mouth and

choked. Susannah and I pounded his back.

"Mom — ," he wheezed, clawing the air. "Mom — " I knew he was in real trouble, calling for his mother like that. What a ghastly way to go, strangling on an anchovy! Then he started babbling about the birds. "Goose," he gasped, pointing.

Suddenly I realized he meant *Mongoose.*

Sure enough, parked by the feeding area was the purple bicycle, with Harry straddling it.

Making a miraculous recovery, Knievel started toward him with Susannah and me.

Susannah pulled us to a halt. "We've got to play it carefully. He might be working with the arsonist. Leave this to me."

She grabbed my arm, and we strolled up beside Harry. Susannah pointed to a skinny-legged bird with white feathers, standing in the pool. "Look, Lucy, there's a heron."

Harry looked down and grinned at her. "Almost. It's an egret — a snowy egret." He wore a sleeveless T-shirt, and I could see the bird tattoo on his arm. "That big one over there is a greater egret."

"Gee." Susannah looked up at him, wide-eyed. "What's the difference between herons and egrets?"

As he explained, I had a feeling Susannah al-

ready knew. "If you want to see herons," Harry said, pointing, "there's a black-crowned night heron."

"Gosh." Susannah looked through the fence. Knievel was gazing worshipfully, too, but not at the heron.

"Terrific bike," he murmured, stroking the fender. "Can't beat a Mongoose. I'd kill for a top-of-the-line one like this."

"Hey, you sound like a guy who knows bikes," said Harry. "Normally I don't let anybody on this baby, but I'll let you try it out. Take it down the road to that clump of trees, but no farther, and don't put any scratches on it, okay?"

"Wow, thanks." Knievel took off like a flash.

"You sure know a lot about birds," Susannah said. "You must spend a lot of time here. Don't you have to work?"

"I'm kind of on vacation. Came out from Michigan with a couple of guys in their bus and decided to stay a while when they moved on."

I almost said, "We know," but caught myself in time.

"I meant to bike up the coast," he went on, "but I'm about out of money. Blew almost every dime I'd saved on the Mongoose. Anyway, it's time I got serious and started college. So I'm heading home tomorrow."

Oh, no, I thought, Susannah better act fast.

She did. "You know," she said, "you remind me of somebody a lady we know told us about. She said he had a bird tattoo like yours and rode a purple Mongoose. He delivered roses to her the other day. That wasn't you, was it?"

I held my breath.

"You're kidding," said Harry. "That sure *was* me. Small world, huh?"

"Really," Susannah agreed. "Mrs. Weinberger would love to know who sent those roses."

"Too bad. She'll just have to keep guessing."

"Huh?" I was dumbfounded.

"I promised the guy not to tell, and I won't."

Knievel skidded up on the Mongoose. "Thanks, that was great."

"You're welcome." Harry took the handlebars. "Well, I better get going."

"Wait." Susannah planted herself in his way. "Please, you've *got* to tell us who sent those roses."

"Look," said Harry, "I don't know his name. Just some guy who stopped me when I was riding around. He gave me fifty bucks to do it, okay?"

"But what did he look like?" I pleaded.

"Come on, kids, quit acting like it's so important." Harry grinned. "It won't kill the lady not to know."

"It might," said Susannah, "if it was her crazy ex-husband, who's threatened to kill her."

"Huh?" Harry's smile faded. "Come on, the guy didn't look like a murderer."

"Most murderers don't," Knievel said darkly. "Was he tall and skinny? Or short and kind of flabby?"

"I forget. Medium, maybe. All I remember is this cool dude in a blue suit and sunglasses and — "

"Blue suit?" I echoed.

"Did he seem nervous?" Susannah asked.

"Not that I noticed," said Harry. "No, I'd say he acted real cool. All business. He handed me the roses and said where to take them. Said to keep ringing till the lady came to the door, not go back to the garden to find her. And to sing 'You Are My Sunshine' when she came." He shook his head. "Told him I sing like one of those ducks over there, but he said it didn't matter and paid me extra to do it."

"That's all you remember about him?" Susannah insisted. "Blue suit, sunglasses, and acting all business. Anything else?"

"Well, the beard, of course."

"Beard?" Susannah and I echoed.

"Yeah, didn't I say? He had a bushy black beard."

⇢ **Chapter 14** ⇠

Before Harry left, Susannah found out where he was camping and got his address in Michigan — just in case.

Then we hiked over to the Leviathan offices on Seventeenth Street. We knew to be careful this time, so we slipped past the fat security guard without his seeing us and took the elevator to the tenth floor.

The receptionist with the long red fingernails frowned as we entered. "You kids back again?"

Susannah turned on her most winning smile. "We'd like to see Mr. — oh, shoot, I forgot his name. He's the one with the black beard."

The woman drummed her fingernails on the desk. "He doesn't work here."

"Oh, no?" Knievel tried to sound menacing.

I jabbed my elbow into his ribs to shut him up.

"No," she said firmly. "The boss has a strict rule: no beards and low-cut dresses."

I giggled, picturing somebody in a beard and a low-cut dress.

"Gee," said Susannah. "Must be another office. Well, thanks."

"But who could the bearded man have been?" Susannah wondered aloud once we got outside. "None of our suspects has a beard."

"Maybe Peterson used to have one and shaved it off." Knievel took a limp candy bar out of his pocket and unwrapped it.

Susannah shook her head. "He was sunburned when we saw him. If he'd just shaved off a beard, the lower part of his face would have been whiter than the rest."

"Oh. Maybe it was fake." Knievel took a huge bite of his candy bar, then offered me some. Looking at the tooth-marked blob, I decided I wasn't hungry.

"Maybe, but if he *was* from Leviathan," I said, "why would they send somebody wearing a beard? People notice beards."

Susannah halted, sucking in her breath. "Interesting idea, Lucy. What if the beard was *meant* to be noticed?"

I blinked. "Why would he want the beard noticed?"

"Because people wouldn't notice much else. Harry couldn't even remember how big he was."

"Right," said Knievel, using his sleeve to wipe chocolate off his face. "Guys with beards look a lot alike."

"And, of course, it's a great way to hide a face somebody might recognize," Susannah added.

I mulled it all over on the way home. Somebody in a false beard had the roses delivered to get Mrs. Weinberger away from her garden while Quiggy's house was set on fire. The arsonist was somebody Rowdy wouldn't bark at. Somebody who had some way to get into the basement. Somebody who knew nobody was home that day. Not a stranger, for sure.

But who wore that black beard? Mr. Peterson? Or maybe Mr. Reid? Or even Ruth?

I was still thinking as we got off the bus near Quiggy's. That's when I remembered I'd promised Pop to take the chicken out of the freezer. Tonight he was making the Chicken Hawaiian he'd bragged about to Knievel's mom. I had to get home fast.

But at the corner by Mr. Reid's house, I heard a scream. It sounded like Theresa.

Then what looked like a string mop streaked by, trailing a red leash and heading toward Mr. Reid's backyard.

"Come back, stupid dog!" Theresa chugged into view. "Don't go in there!"

But Pipsqueak squirmed under the gate into Mr. Reid's backyard, where Rowdy barked ferociously.

"Get that silly thing out of there!" Mr. Reid, who'd been opening his mailbox on the front porch, came running. "Rowdy'll make hamburger meat out of him!"

We ran. Knievel and I beat Theresa to the gate. We both clawed at the latch, while inside Rowdy snarled and Pipsqueak whimpered. Then suddenly it was silent.

I tore through the gate and stopped. The dogs were circling each other, sniffing. Then, half doubtfully, Rowdy's tail began to twitch. Pipsqueak's stirred, too. The next moment, they were wagging their rear ends off.

"Aw," I said, "they just want to play."

Mr. Reid's face went an angry red. "Get that ridiculous animal out of my yard before I . . ."

Theresa scooped up Pipsqueak and struggled

to hold him while Rowdy pawed at her, whining. "Stop squirming, Pipsqueak, you hateful thing." She glanced at Susannah. "I've got to get him home before Ruth comes back. Come with me — I've got to tell you something important."

→ **Chapter 15** ←

It was Theresa's unlucky day. Just as we reached Quiggy's front door, I saw Ruth hurrying up the street.

"Put down my dog, you little monster!" she shrieked.

Theresa spilled Pipsqueak out of her arms. "Take the stupid mutt!"

Quiggy must have heard the shouting, because she opened the front door. "Now, Ruth," she said soothingly, "Pipsqueak was making such a fuss, Theresa offered to walk him."

"She's not supposed to touch him." Clutching the dog, Ruth hurried into the hall and started up the stairs.

"You think I *wanted* to walk your dumb dog?" Theresa yelled after her.

Toby appeared in the doorway to the kitchen. He looked great in his paint-splattered overalls. I wanted to ignore him after the way he'd acted in the building downtown, but then he grinned and winked at me. I couldn't help grinning back.

"I need your key to the outside basement door, Aunt Quig," he said. "Mine's on that key chain I lost. I need a flashlight, too. Got to borrow the longer ladder from down there for a few minutes."

"Why not use the hallway stairs?" asked Quiggy.

"Just painted the door, that's why."

"I'll get the key." Quiggy started up the stairs. "The flashlight's in that drawer, under the phone."

"Sorry to be a bother, Aunt Quig," Toby called after her. "Can't think what I did with those keys."

Susannah looked interested. "When did you lose them?"

"That day I helped Theresa move in." Toby rummaged through the drawer of the phone table and took out the flashlight. "Luckily, I've got another set, except for the key to the basement."

The doorbell rang. Knievel answered it.

"Yes, monsieur?" He bowed like a butler. Only butlers don't usually wear chocolate-stained T-shirts.

Monsieur Reid didn't find him funny. "Miss Quigley!" he bellowed. "I've had all I'm going to take of these brats!"

Quiggy hurried downstairs and handed her key chain to Toby. "What's wrong now, Mr. Reid?"

What was wrong was that he'd locked himself out of his house when he went chasing after Pipsqueak. And somehow that was all our fault.

"All I need," Mr. Reid growled, "is your phone to call my brother. He's got a key to my house."

"By all means," Quiggy said politely. "Then make yourself comfortable in the living room. You children come help me fix coffee."

As we followed her into the kitchen, she whispered, "Try to excuse his manners. He's really a nice man under all that gruffness."

While she made coffee, Susannah, Theresa, and I helped by putting cups and napkins on a tray, and Knievel taste-tested the cookies.

Quiggy shook her finger at him, smiling. "There's a box of cookies for you kids, and milk in the refrigerator."

As she picked up the tray, Toby returned from the basement and handed her the keys. Quiggy invited him to join her and Mr. Reid for coffee in the living room.

"You children can come, too, if you want," she added.

There was nothing I wanted more than to follow Toby into the living room, but Susannah grabbed my arm.

"Now," Susannah said when the kitchen door closed behind Quiggy and Toby, "what's up, Theresa?"

"I found out Ruth wasn't with Quiggy the day the porch caught fire."

Susannah's eyebrows rose. "You sure?"

"This morning Quiggy was talking about the movie I didn't get to see. She said it was so bad, Ruth left right after it started. She met Quiggy back at the car when it was over."

"Hmm." Susannah frowned over her glasses. "You know, that man with the false beard *could* have been a woman."

"Sure," said Knievel, "I bet Ruth had time to dress like a man, put on a beard, and meet Harry."

"Then get back here and set the fire," I said.

"Beard? Harry? What are you talking about?" Theresa demanded.

Susannah frowned. "To do all that and get back before the movie was over, she'd have to take a taxi or Quiggy's car or —"

"Or Peterson's car," said Knievel. "Bet he was waiting for her in his yellow Datsun when she came out of the movie."

"Yeah," I said. "Or maybe he did it and Ruth helped. Anyway, they could have planned the whole thing together."

"That old witch!" Theresa gritted her teeth. "I bet she started the fight with me in the car just so I'd use bad words and Quiggy would send me home. Then everybody would think I set the fire to get even."

"Yeah," said Knievel. "Getting you blamed for the fire was part of the plan. Right, Susannah?"

Susannah nodded. "That makes sense. But some other parts of the puzzle don't fit."

Glancing at my watch, I saw it was nearly five. Too late to defrost the chicken before Pop got home. I leaped up.

"I've got to phone Pop!" There was just time to catch him at work and tell him he'd better pick up pizza.

"And I've got to call Mom!" Knievel squawked. "I promised to be home by five.

We're going to your house for something barfy called Chicken Hawaiian."

"The menu's just been changed to Chicken Antarctica," I called back as I dived through the door and out to the hall.

There stood Ruth. Clearly, she'd been eavesdropping at the door to the living room, where Mr. Reid and Toby were having coffee with Quiggy. I didn't think she could have heard us.

Glaring at me, she said, "I was looking for Pipsqueak's toy." Then she hurried upstairs.

When I got Pop on the phone, he didn't actually blow up. He just said that he'd take Mae out to dinner and a movie. Knievel and I could eat TV dinners.

"We'll eat at Susannah's," I told him. We hadn't been invited, but Mrs. Higgins was used to our staying for dinner. "Pick us up there after the movie, okay?"

Susannah, Theresa, and Knievel had followed me into the hall. Just as I turned to tell Susannah she'd invited us to dinner, the doorbell rang. Knievel opened the front door.

Mr. Peterson almost fell into the hall. He must have been leaning against the door.

Quiggy hurried from the living room to see who it was.

"What are *you* doing here?" She looked cross.

"Please, Miss Quigley," Mr. Peterson begged, "you really must listen."

"Yes, listen to him." Mr. Reid got up from his chair in the living room. "God knows why, but he wants to buy this old place for more than it's worth. You'll be a rich woman."

Quiggy looked at Mr. Reid. "And you'll be rich, too, because then he'll buy your house."

"Well, yes, but . . ." He sat back down. "Sure, I'll benefit when you sell. So will Mrs. Weinberger."

I heard a noise behind me. Ruth was hurrying downstairs. Her eyes darted from Theresa to Mr. Peterson. Brushing Knievel aside, she stopped in front of Quiggy.

"You're going to sell the house?"

"Now don't worry, dear," Quiggy said quickly.

"On the contrary," growled Mr. Reid, "she *should* worry that you're passing up a small fortune for this old barn."

Ruth gazed at Quiggy, breathing hard. "Sell it."

Quiggy looked stunned.

"But . . . but I thought you loved this house, Ruth."

"I do. But it's awfully big, and wouldn't we be happier in a nice condo on a beach somewhere? We could afford something really nice with the money you get for the house. A small place, just room for us two." She shot a venomous look at Theresa, who was standing behind me with Susannah.

Mr. Peterson beamed. "See, Miss Quigley? Your cousin agrees you should sell. I bet your nephew does, too, right?"

Toby, leaning on the back of a chair, shrugged. "Sounds like a good idea to me, Aunt Quig."

Quiggy stood very still, looking at her folded hands.

"You're right," she said finally. "I'd be foolish not to sell. This old house is out-of-date. Who'll care when Leviathan tears it down to build a fancy high rise? Oh, yes, Mr. Peterson, I can guess who the real buyer is."

I felt sick. After all the trouble we'd gone to, Quiggy was going to sell the house after all.

"Who cares that my grandparents built this house and my mother was born here? Who'll miss the old-fashioned living room with ceilings so high you need a tall ladder to reach them? Who cares if they tear it down?"

Nobody answered, but I heard Ruth take a sharp breath.

"Well, I'll tell you who cares." Quiggy lifted her chin. "I do. This is my home and I want to live here, not in the finest condo there is. I'm sorry, Mr. Peterson, you'll have to tell Leviathan I'm just a foolish woman who won't sell my home — not at *any* price. Now, more coffee, anyone?"

The way she said it, even Mr. Peterson didn't try to argue. He left looking furious. Mr. Reid went off snorting, "Women! They've got no brains for financial matters."

What a sexist, I thought. I'll bet he doesn't have half Quiggy's brain for finances.

We hung around in the hall while Ruth begged Quiggy to change her mind.

"Please, Quig. We could travel around the world together . . . do anything we want. Just the two of us, the way it used to be."

But Quiggy only shook her head. Finally Ruth gave up and flounced upstairs, skirting Theresa as if she were a mud puddle.

It was nearly six o'clock when we left. Susannah turned to Theresa as we went out the door.

"Keep your eyes open. Phone me if . . .

well, if you see anything wrong." She sounded worried.

We headed for Susannah's house, huddling in our jackets. The late-afternoon sun had snuggled into a blanket of fog, and a chilly wind was rising, chillier than usual for this time of year.

Susannah scowled as we hurried along.

"What's the matter?" I asked.

She gave me a strange look. "I think there's going to be another fire — soon. Maybe tonight."

→ Chapter 16 ←

"*Tonight?*" Knievel and I echoed.

"Could be." Susannah chewed her lip. "Quiggy's made it clear she really won't sell the house, and the arsonist knows it. I better tell Grandpa. He'll know how to handle this."

But the note on the dining-room table said her grandparents had gone out to dinner.

"Darn, I forgot," said Susannah, "and your folks won't be picking you up till late. But we need adult help *now*. The police won't listen to us without any evidence."

"You know who the arsonist is?" I asked.

"Not for sure." She turned to Knievel. "Can you climb that tree outside my bedroom window?"

"I can climb *anything*." For once, he wasn't bragging. Knievel is half monkey. "Why?"

"Because you can see Quiggy's from the top branches. The least we can do is keep watch on her house till Grandpa gets home."

"The least *I* can do, you mean," Knievel said sourly. "Okay, but dinner first. I'm starving."

"You'll have to eat on the job, Jones. Nobody ever said an operative's life was easy."

Grumbling, Knievel made himself a sandwich from the meat loaf in the refrigerator. He squashed it in his jacket pocket and went out to climb the tree.

Susannah and I took our dinner up to her room and sprawled on her bed by the window. From there we could see Knievel perched in the tree.

It was just past six-thirty, when the sky should still have been bright. But tonight it was like winter twilight. The chill wind was the kind you get before a storm. Only it almost never rains here in the summer.

I munched my meat loaf while time dragged by and the sky grew darker. Knievel's tree began tossing. It must have felt like whitewater rafting.

Susannah frowned at the ceiling and grunted when I tried to start conversation, so I just stared at her snake pictures.

It was past eight o'clock when I heard distant sirens, then Knievel's earsplitting whistle. Susannah and I raced to the window.

Across the rooftops, an orange sky flickered behind Quiggy's high attic window. The cold wind smelled of smoke. The sirens wailed louder, nearer.

Susannah and I tore downstairs, out the front door, and down the blocks to Quiggy's. We raced around the corner by Mr. Reid's house and stopped, bewildered.

Quiggy's house wasn't on fire. It stood thin and dignified against the orange sky, the windows dark. The lights and shouting came from behind it.

"Mrs. Weinberger's house!" Susannah gasped.

We dashed around the corner by Mr. Reid's to the street behind. There a policeman was waving cars away. Rubber-suited figures ran from fire trucks with ladders and hoses.

Smoke poured out of Mrs. Weinberger's basement windows, scattering sparks into the wind.

I looked at Susannah, frightened. "Mrs. Weinberger . . . ?"

She wasn't among the people clustered on

the sidewalk, and nobody had seen her. Then we spotted Toby and ran over.

"Have you seen Mrs. Weinberger?" Susannah asked.

"No." He pushed up the collar of his new-looking black leather jacket against the wind. "Look, you girls better go home. The fire fighters don't need kids getting in their way."

Which reminded me to wonder where Knievel had gotten to.

More neighbors came running to watch, some in their bathrobes. The wind hurled showers of sparks high in the air. Across the street, a man sprayed water from a garden hose on his roof so it wouldn't catch fire.

Mr. Reid scurried up, clutching his bathrobe around him.

"Go move that pile of lumber out of the yard!" he yelled at Toby. "The wind's blowing sparks back there. If Miss Quigley's house catches fire, it'll spread to mine."

"Better clean that trash out of your own yard," Toby retorted. "It's more likely to catch fire than the lumber."

I saw Susannah staring at the crowd across the street. Mr. Peterson was there, jingling his pockets.

Then we spotted Theresa hugging herself against the wind.

"Have you seen Mrs. Weinberger?" I demanded.

"No." Her eyes widened. "You don't think she's in — "

"Where's Quiggy?" Susannah asked. "And Ruth?"

"Quiggy went to a friend's after dinner. I don't know where Ruth is. I was watching TV when I heard the sirens."

"We'd better call Quiggy," Susannah said. "Did she leave her friend's phone number?"

Quiggy had, of course. Susannah insisted on going back to the house with Theresa. I didn't see why until Susannah said we'd have a better view of the fire from one of Quiggy's upstairs rooms.

"We can look down and keep an eye on the suspects," she said as we raced back around the corner, dodging people coming to watch the fire.

We already had an eye on one suspect, for ahead of us Mr. Reid scurried home, his bathrobe ballooning behind him. As he passed his fence, Rowdy quit yowling and gave welcoming barks.

But Pipsqueak was still yelping upstairs as

Theresa unlocked Quiggy's front door. Bursting into the hallway, I took deep breaths of the clean air inside.

Theresa headed upstairs. "You call Quiggy while I get my jacket. I'm freezing. The number's on the pad by the phone."

"Lucy," Susannah said as she punched in the number, "go look out upstairs and see what's happening at the fire."

I followed Theresa upstairs. Behind Ruth's door, Pipsqueak yipped and scratched to get out.

"Shut up, you yappy mutt!" Theresa yelled as she ran to the ladder to her attic room.

I opened the door to Quiggy's room, which faced the backyard. A blast of smoky wind whipped me. It was dark inside, except for the glow through the curtains billowing in the window. I patted the wall, hunting for the light switch.

Something felt wrong. My eyes flickered over the bed and dresser, then back to the window. Yes, that was where I'd seen something move, and not just the curtains.

Then I saw it again — a pair of white gloves inching along the windowsill.

→ Chapter 17 ←

The hands vanished — so fast I almost thought I'd imagined them.

My heart thudding, I stood frozen a minute. Then I cautiously approached the window and peered out. Below, tossing bushes sent shadows darting around the backyard. Was one of the shadows somebody running?

I heard Susannah coming upstairs and ran to meet her.

"Somebody tried to climb in Quiggy's window."

"*Who?*"

"I just saw the hands. Whoever it was is gone now."

I followed her to the window.

Susannah scanned the backyard. "Hmm.

Must have just opened the window, heard you, and left."

I thought. "You know, I think he — or she — was already leaving when I got here."

Sparks were flying toward us on the wind, and the smoke made me cough. Then I caught another smell.

Susannah sniffed. "Gasoline! Somebody's set fire to the lumber pile." She slammed down the window. "Let's get out of here before the house catches fire. Where's Theresa?"

We raced into the hall. "Theresa!" I bellowed.

She probably couldn't hear me over Pipsqueak's yelping. I clambered up the ladder to the attic.

"Run!" I shrieked. "The lumber pile's on fire!"

Theresa stared at me.

"Come *on!*"

Downstairs Susannah yelled to hurry.

Theresa ran to the closet and yanked clothes off hangers. "Get my new bedspread, Lucy, and — "

"There isn't time. Come on!"

Susannah burst in. She grabbed Theresa's arm and towed her to the door. Theresa stumbled along, clutching a bundle of clothes.

"Wait, my skates are under the bed!"

"You want to burn up? Move, girl!"

The smell of smoke in the hall must have convinced Theresa. She clambered down the ladder, and I followed.

Susannah flung Ruth's door open as we passed. "Run, Pipsqueak!" she yelled.

At the end of the hall we stopped. The fire must have spread to the inside. A cloud of smoke rolled up the stairs. We were trapped.

Susannah yanked her sweatshirt up over her nose. I did the same with my shirt, remembering that breathing smoke is mostly what kills people in fires. Theresa clutched her bundle of clothes to her face. Coughing, we retreated back the way we'd come.

"Stay low," Susannah wheezed through her sweatshirt, crouching as she ran. "Smoke rises — there's less near the floor. And keep calm. We'll climb out a window."

Quiggy's and Ruth's rooms were useless. If we jumped out those windows, we'd land on the burning lumber. Pipsqueak stood yowling piteously in Ruth's doorway. Poor mutt didn't know where else to go.

We tried the bathroom across the hall, but the tiny window over the tub wouldn't budge.

Neither did the windows in the spare bedroom. Smoke stung my eyes, and I couldn't stop coughing. I forced my teary eyes open and squinted at the watery blur.

"The attic," Susannah wheezed.

It was our only chance. Crouching low, I stumbled toward the ladder.

Behind me, Susannah croaked, "Theresa, come here!"

Squinting back, I saw Theresa dump her precious belongings outside Ruth's door and dash in. Was she crazy?

I couldn't worry about her. It was all I could do to get up the ladder, with my head woozy and my legs like rubber. When I reached the top, I heard a whimper behind me.

At the foot of the ladder, Theresa cradled Pipsqueak in her arms. She handed him up to me, then climbed.

We burst into Theresa's room, slammed the door, and raced to the window.

Even before I looked down into the front yard, I knew it was too far to jump. And the spiky iron fence was below.

"Help!" we yelled. "Help!" again and again.

The street was empty, the houses on the other side dark.

"Everybody's at the fire at Mrs. Weinberger's!" Theresa gasped. "What'll we do?"

"We'll have to climb down." Susannah said that so calmly, you'd never guess she's afraid of heights.

"Right," I said. It would be tricky — a fifteen-foot drop just to the windowsill below. "We need a rope."

Susannah was already yanking sheets off Theresa's bed and knotting them together. Theresa, getting the idea, started to tie one end to the leg of her desk.

I snatched it from her. "Not heavy enough. We'll pull it out the window behind us." I tied one end of the rope of sheets to a leg of her dresser, then dropped the other end out the window. It dangled only midway to the ground.

I yanked it back and tied on Theresa's bedspread. This time the end reached the living-room window. We'd jump from there and hope not to land on the sharp spikes of the fence.

I hauled up the rope and checked the knots. I may not be our leader's favorite Girl Scout, but I'm the only one who's earned a knot-tying badge.

"Who's first?" I asked.

Theresa took a step back.

"I'll be first." Susannah sat down on the windowsill. Sweat dotted her forehead. "Sure hope those knots hold."

"Me too." My palms were so clammy I could hardly tie the rope around her waist. I double-checked the knots as she straddled the windowsill and eased one leg out into space.

"Jump wide of that iron fence when you let go of the rope." I leaned out the window to point.

I heard a noise overhead and looked up. Hanging over the edge of the roof above was a face.

→ **Chapter 18** ←

Knievel squinted down from the roof a few feet above, his hair plastered back by the wind. He must have climbed up there to watch the fire at Mrs. Weinberger's and then heard our voices.

"Hey, you better get out of there," he advised. "Smoke's pouring out of a window downstairs. I'm getting down." His face disappeared.

"Come back!" I yelped. Theresa started shrieking.

"Jones!" bellowed Susannah. "We're trapped!"

Knievel's face reappeared. "I'll go for help."

"No!" I yelled. "Help us get on the roof."

I knew he'd climbed up the tree on the

other side of the roof, by the kitchen. That was the safest way down.

Susannah wriggled out of the loop around her waist. "Jones, tie this to the chimney. Theresa, help me untie the other end."

I flung the loop up to Knievel. The wind blew it out of his reach. I tried again. He missed again.

"Won't work," he yelled. "I'll go get help."

"Wait!" I needed something to weight the rope. I yanked off my sneaker and tied it by the laces to the sheet.

Behind me, Susannah and Theresa struggled to undo the knot around the dresser leg. From under the bed came Pipsqueak's terrified yowls.

I pitched the shoe to Knievel. He caught it.

I ran to help Susannah and Theresa. The knot was hopeless, so they lifted the dresser while I slipped the rope off.

"Time to go, Susannah." I slid the rope under her arms and tested the knot. Knievel shouted that his end was around the chimney. I prayed his knots were as good as mine.

"Don't look down," I warned as she eased one foot out the window.

She clenched her teeth and began pulling

herself up. The sheets strained with her weight, but the knots held.

She made it over the edge of the roof. I started breathing again. Moments later she dropped the end of the rope back to me. I turned to Theresa.

Her feet stuck out from under the bed.

"What are you doing?" Did she think she could take her roller skates with her?

But it wasn't skates she pulled out. It was Pipsqueak.

"No," I said. "You need both hands for climbing."

Theresa clutched the tiny dog. "I can't leave him here to die." Pipsqueak snuggled against her, whimpering.

"Hurry up!" Knievel shouted from the roof.

There wasn't time to argue. "Where's your backpack?"

Theresa ran to get it. We zipped Pipsqueak inside. He struggled wildly.

"Leave him to me," I said. "I'll tie the backpack to the rope as soon as you're up."

"No," she said. "Pipsqueak comes with me."

Susannah and Knievel kept shouting to hurry.

"Okay, it's your funeral." I looped the rope around Theresa's waist.

She climbed onto the windowsill, glanced down, and shivered. Then, taking a deep breath, she began hauling herself up. At the overhang she stopped, waiting for the backpack to quit heaving before she let go of the rope to grab the ledge.

"Do it!" Knievel pleaded. "The loop will catch you if you fall."

He couldn't help her. If he gave her a hand, she'd pull him over. But somehow he talked her over the ledge and onto the roof.

I caught the loop, slipped it under my arms, and stepped into space. I hauled myself up to the overhang and clambered onto the roof. But there was no time to relax.

"We've got to get down from here," said Susannah. "The roof might cave in."

I squirmed on my belly after the others, down the peak of the attic to the gentler slope at the back of the house. My palms scraped painfully on the rough shingles. I longed to stop and blow on them. It must have been even worse for Susannah, with her fear of heights.

It was dark now, except for the glow of

floodlights from Mrs. Weinberger's house beyond the backyard, as we crawled down the endless hill of the roof.

"There's the tree," Knievel called.

We'd reached the flat part at the back. On the side by Mr. Reid's house, a thick branch nearly touched the roof — a ladder to the ground.

I scrambled to my feet, then stopped.

The tree had caught fire. Flames rippled along the branch onto the roof.

→ Chapter 19 ←

"Help!" we yelled. "Help!"

We scurried away from the burning branch. We'd never get down *that* tree. I crawled on my belly, toward the edge of the roof over the backyard. But there smoke billowed up from the lumber pile.

"This way!" Susannah scrambled on hands and knees to the far side of the roof, and Theresa crawled behind her. Knievel and I slid after them and peered over the edge. Not too smoky here, but a long drop to the ground.

I heard a shout. "Fire! The house is on fire!"

"Help!" we screamed.

"Good Lord! Those kids are up there!" I heard Toby's voice. Then I saw him running through the haze.

"Don't jump! It's too far," he yelled. "I'll get the tall ladder from the basement."

A minute later he slammed a ladder against the house. I always knew someday Toby would be my hero.

"Hurry!" He coughed as smoke blew over him.

Theresa started down first, balancing her squirming backpack. Susannah went next, then Knievel. By the time I touched ground, the others were sprinting toward the back hedge.

"Run, everybody!" Susannah yelled. "We've got to get the fire fighters here fast!"

I raced to catch up, tripped, and sprawled on my stomach. I got to my feet, but my left ankle hurt. I rubbed it. Didn't feel sprained, but I sure couldn't run on it.

I felt suddenly alone. The voices across the hedge seemed far away, lost in the whispers of the wind through the shrubbery. The flicker of the burning lumber pile sent eerie shadows darting about the yard.

There were footsteps behind me. Before I could turn, an arm clamped my waist.

"Come with me, kid." I knew that harsh voice.

I struggled, but he pinned my arms tight.

"Calm down!" he ordered, but I kept kicking and yelling.

He picked me up, smothering my yells against his shirt.

I didn't know where he was taking me, but I knew why. Because on his hands I saw white gloves.

He must have known I'd seen him in Quiggy's window. So now Mr. Reid had to get rid of me.

He pinned my legs so I couldn't kick. There was only one thing to do. I went limp.

Mr. Reid scrabbled to catch me as I slithered to the ground. The next second I was up, kicking and slugging.

"Let her go!" a voice yelped from behind. Knievel dived, toppling Mr. Reid onto me. I struggled out from under him, sucking in air.

"You okay, Lucy?" Knievel straddled Mr. Reid. "I wondered where you'd got to, so — "

"Get off me, you hoodlum!" Mr. Reid tried to buck Knievel off.

I sat down on him, too. "Thanks," I wheezed. "Next time, try not to squash me, huh, Knievel?"

"Quit complaining," said Knievel. "At least we caught the arsonist."

"Get off him!" Susannah hurried around the corner of the house. "Mr. Reid isn't the arsonist."

"You crazy?" I gaped at her. "He nearly killed me."

"So that's the thanks I get for saving your life." Mr. Reid struggled to get up.

"Saving my life?" I sputtered. "You were kidnapping me."

"Kidnapping! I was getting you away from the fire. I saw you over the fence. You were too frightened to run."

"Oh, yeah? Then how come you wouldn't let me go when I kicked and yelled?" But Knievel and I let him get up.

"You were obviously hysterical," Mr. Reid said.

"Hysterical! *Me?*" That was too much. Knievel's giggles didn't help my feelings.

"I thought I'd better get you to safety," Mr. Reid said righteously. "Some thanks I get for my kindness."

Susannah helped him brush off his bathrobe. "I think you *were* just trying to help, Mr. Reid. Quiggy says you're a kind man underneath your gruffness."

"Susannah," I said, "he's wearing those gloves."

Fire fighters raced into Quiggy's front yard. "Get those kids out of here!" one shouted.

I wanted to get indoors anyway. The wind

was dying down, but the air was chilly.

"You can go sit in my kitchen," Mr. Reid said grumpily. "I've got to finish moving the trash pile so it doesn't catch fire." He unlocked his door for us and hurried off.

"Susannah," I said, "he's the one I saw in Quiggy's window. Those white gardening gloves . . ."

"Of course he's wearing gardening gloves. He was cleaning up his trash."

"So he says, but —"

"Come on, Lucy. Mr. Reid is way too out of shape to shinny up to Quiggy's window."

"You've got a point," said Knievel. "But don't forget that lighter-fluid can we found in his yard."

"That's another reason I don't think he's the arsonist. Would *you* set a fire next door and throw the evidence in your own backyard?"

"You mean somebody put it there so he'd be blamed?"

"Right," said Susannah.

I thought that over. "But if it wasn't Mr. Reid . . ."

"Just a minute," said Susannah. "I've got to go to the bathroom, then make a phone call."

Knievel beat me to second turn at the bathroom. I was just coming out as Susannah hung up the phone by the refrigerator. Then the back door opened. Quiggy hurried in, followed by Theresa.

"Theresa told me what happened. Thank heaven you're all safe." Quiggy hugged Susannah and me. Knievel ducked as she turned toward him.

Toby followed Theresa in. "They sure had me scared when I saw them up on the roof," he said. "Lucky I remembered that tall ladder in the basement."

Behind Toby I saw Mrs. Weinberger.

"They've saved my house," she said joyfully.

The door opened again, and Ruth hurried in out of the chilly night with Pipsqueak squirming in her arms and Rowdy following. Mr. Reid closed the door behind them, looking put out at all the uninvited company.

"What about *your* house?" Susannah asked Quiggy. "Can they save it?"

"I hope so," said Quiggy. "They don't think the fire's spread upstairs, though there's lots of smoke."

"You kids got the fire fighters to Quiggy's just in time," said Toby. He looked great in his black leather jacket.

"You sure did," said Quiggy. "Apparently the lumber pile caught fire, set the tree afire, and then sparks ignited something in the downstairs hall. What bad luck!"

"Not bad luck," said Susannah. "Somebody deliberately set fire to that lumber, then opened your bedroom window to let the smoke in. Then this person set a fire in the downstairs hall."

Quiggy's jaw knotted angrily. "Leviathan."

"Someone working for Leviathan, all right," said Susannah. "The same person who set the porch on fire. Somebody who knew nobody was home that day and had a way to get in."

Ruth stopped petting Pipsqueak. "What do you mean?"

"She means you," I said. "You left Quiggy at the movies that day, changed into a man's suit and a beard, got Harry to deliver roses to Mrs. Weinberger — "

"Harry who?" Mrs. Weinberger looked bewildered.

" — then came back and set the fire," Knievel finished.

"Ruth! *You* did it?" Toby looked at her.

"This is insane!" Ruth gasped. "Why would I try to burn down the house?"

"Good question," said Susannah. "Even if you wanted Quiggy to sell it, you'd be crazy to set it on fire. Leviathan wouldn't have to pay as much for an empty lot."

I felt confused. "It wasn't Ruth?"

Susannah shook her head. "Think about it. Would Ruth have set fire to the house tonight with Pipsqueak inside?"

"But we saw her talking to Peterson," Knievel argued, "and this afternoon she begged Quiggy to sell him the house."

"It wasn't that way." Ruth turned anxiously to Quiggy. "That awful man *did* try to talk to me at the BART station. Had the gall to offer me money to get you to sell." Her mouth twisted angrily. "I gave him a piece of my mind. But later I got to thinking about all the money you'd get for the house, and that maybe you'd be happier somewhere else."

"Was it really me you were thinking of?" Quiggy asked quietly.

Ruth stroked Pipsqueak a minute. "Well, both of us," she said. "If we moved away, you couldn't take Theresa. You didn't tell me she has to leave anyway." She glanced at Theresa almost shyly. "Sorry. I guess I've been unfair to you. Thanks for saving Pipsqueak's life."

Theresa shrugged. She looked as if she wasn't used to having people apologize to her.

"Anyway," said Susannah, "the question is, who — "

Mr. Peterson poked his head in the back door.

"Oh, there you are, Miss Quigley." He straightened his tie. "I'm sorry about your house, but looks like they've licked the fire before it did too much damage."

"Nice timing, Peterson," Knievel said. "We were just thinking about you."

Mr. Peterson's smile froze. "What do you mean?"

Susannah looked at him sternly. "I think you can forget about buying houses and selling them back to Leviathan."

"Yeah," I said. "And you won't get another chance to burn them down either."

"What?" He stumbled against the counter. "Now wait a minute, I didn't set those fires."

"Oh, no?" Toby muttered.

Mr. Peterson's eyes darted around the people staring at him. "Look, I'm a real-estate agent. Leviathan wants to tear down these houses and build high rises, and they don't want stupid people who are against progress to make trouble. So Leviathan hired me to buy the houses. Then I sell them to Leviathan at a profit." He ran a hand through his hair, then jingled his pocket.

"I thought so." Susannah nodded. "I never could quite picture you setting fires. The only real reason we suspected you was that match we saw you holding. But I guess you just meant to light a cigarette."

I stared at her. "But it had to be him. He's even wearing the blue suit Harry saw him in."

Susannah shrugged. "People can change their clothes easier than their habits. The man Harry saw didn't seem at all nervous. Can you see Mr. Peterson being cool and calm — not even jingling his pockets — when he's going to set fire to Quiggy's house?"

I looked at Mr. Peterson shakily lighting a cigarette. "No way," I admitted. "And anyway, how could Peterson get into the house without a key?"

We were running out of suspects.

"Then who *is* the arsonist?" Knievel demanded.

There was only one person left.

I looked at Theresa. She began to cry.

⇢ **Chapter 20** ⇠

"I didn't do it!" Theresa shrieked. "I didn't!"

Ruth stared at her, and Toby shook his head sadly.

Quiggy wrapped her arms around Theresa. "I know you didn't, darling."

I hated to tell Quiggy, but somebody had to. "The fires started right after Theresa came. And she's set fires before."

Quiggy turned on me, furious. "How dare you! For your information, I know all about the fire at the Featherstones', and the school, too. The agency told me before I took her."

"You *knew?*" Theresa looked stunned.

"Of course, precious." Quiggy hugged her tightly. "But anybody who says you set fire to my house —"

"Not me," said Susannah. "Theresa didn't do it."

I felt strangely relieved.

"But Susannah," said Knievel, "Theresa and Ruth are the only ones who had keys to the front door the day the porch caught fire."

"Yes, but the arsonist got in through the basement."

"How?" Knievel demanded. "Quiggy had the only key."

"You forget something, fuzz-brain," I said. I'd just remembered it myself. "Toby lost his key to the basement. The arsonist must have stolen it."

"Good Lord!" Toby snapped his fingers. "I bet you're right."

Susannah peered at Toby. "That might explain it, except for one thing. If you didn't have the key, how did you unlock the basement to get the ladder tonight?"

The room went very quiet.

"And why did you ask for a flashlight to go down to the basement this afternoon?" Susannah's voice was deadly calm. "Unless you knew the light had burned out."

I couldn't believe what she was saying. But I stared at the white gardening gloves sticking out of the pocket of his leather jacket.

"Toby is the arsonist?" asked Knievel.

"I'm afraid so," said Susannah.

Toby plunged out the door. Two cops were waiting. They hustled him off to a patrol car fast.

Knowing Susannah, I shouldn't have been surprised that she'd phoned the police arson detail while I was in the bathroom earlier.

I felt as sick as Quiggy looked.

"I always suspected Toby was getting all that money dishonestly." She shook her head sadly. "He's just too slick for his own good."

It was after ten before we had time to talk, sitting in Susannah's kitchen. We'd arrived in a patrol car, after being checked over by the paramedics and quizzed by the fire marshal. By then they'd put out the fire in Quiggy's house and said the house might last another hundred years.

Back at Susannah's, we got hugged and scolded and hugged some more by her grandparents. But finally they'd left us in the kitchen with cocoa and cookies to wait for Pop and Mae to pick up Knievel and me.

I didn't think I wanted to talk about what had happened. It hurt too much. But my curiosity got the best of me.

"When did you start suspecting Toby worked for Leviathan?" I asked Susannah.

She gulped her cocoa and poured more. "When we saw him in that building where Leviathan's offices are. He claimed he'd just had a tooth pulled, but he didn't talk like his mouth was numb from Novacain. But the real tip-off was when he asked for the flashlight this afternoon."

I remembered Theresa's saying the light was on when she'd been down there with Toby to store the stuff from the attic. "The bulb must have burned out when he came through to set the porch on fire."

"Exactly." Susannah put her feet on the table. It was a good thing her grandmother wasn't there to see her. "Toby wanted Quiggy to think he'd lost his key, so she wouldn't suspect him. He hoped she'd blame Theresa for the fire."

Knievel, having polished off the cookies, went to look in the refrigerator. "You mean Toby knew about Theresa and that fire at the Featherstones'?"

"I'm sure he did," Susannah said. "Quiggy probably told him when she was thinking of taking in Theresa. She probably wanted to talk it over with somebody, but not Ruth, who'd have had a fit."

"I bet Toby told her to take in Theresa," I said, forcing myself to face facts. "She'd come in handy to take the blame for him."

"Yeah," said Knievel. "But how did he know Theresa got sent home that day he set the porch on fire?"

Susannah shrugged. "Probably saw her playing in the park when he drove by. Knowing Quiggy and Ruth were at the movies, he decided the time was ripe. All he had to do was make sure Mrs. Weinberger didn't see him get in through the basement. And that's where Harry and his purple Mongoose came in."

Knievel took a container out of the freezer, smiling happily. "Ice cream."

"Frozen yogurt," said Susannah. "I'll settle for that."

"Me too." I snatched the carton before Knievel could get his grubby fingers into it. "But what was Ruth up to, always nosing around and watching us?"

Susannah rocked dangerously back in her chair. "Trying to get something on Theresa — to convince Quiggy she was bad. That's why she'd been searching Theresa's room that time we saw her coming down from the attic. She snooped on us because we're Theresa's friends."

That made me feel guilty. I hadn't been much of a friend to Theresa.

"Maybe Ruth isn't so bad really," I said. "She was just jealous of Theresa, like an only child with a new sister."

"Let's hope she feels more sisterly now," Susannah said, "after Theresa went to all that trouble to save Pipsqueak."

"Tell me something." Knievel finished off his dish of frozen yogurt and helped himself again. "Why didn't Toby burn the house down in the first place instead of just setting fire to the garage and the porch?"

"Because he cares about Quiggy," said Susannah. "I think he kept hoping to scare her into selling. Even tonight, when he was getting desperate, he set a fire that wouldn't do much damage if the fire department arrived in time."

Knievel scraped out the carton and upended it over his mouth to get the last dribble. "He set fire to Mrs. Weinberger's house to scare her into selling, too?"

"Yes, but also so the fire fighters would be nearby when he set fire to Quiggy's house."

I sighed. "Toby isn't really a terrible person. He didn't know we were in the house when he set it on fire."

"No," said Susannah, "he didn't mean to kill us. But he nearly did."

"Yeah," said Knievel, "and it was rotten trying to lay the blame on Theresa for those other fires."

"Still," I said, "when he got the ladder out of the basement, he blew his alibi to save us." I couldn't bear to think there was nothing good about him.

Nobody argued with that.

The next day an article in the *Tribune* said that Toby's confession had led to the arrest of the Leviathan Corporation's officers. There was another article with a picture of Quiggy and Ruth with their arms around Theresa, who was holding Pipsqueak. It was titled *Happy Foster Family*.

I felt cheated. The paper didn't mention that we'd solved the case.

A few days later Quiggy asked Susannah, Knievel, and me to come over. She said she had another surprise.

"Come back to the kitchen," she said when she opened the front door. "I've got people knocking down plaster in the hall. In fact, while I'm having the damage repaired, I'm getting the whole place rewired, as Mr. Reid recommended."

It felt sad that Toby wouldn't be helping with the work.

"This is Mr. Gonzalez," she said as we trooped into the kitchen, where Theresa and a tall man were waiting. "He has something to tell you."

"First," said Mr. Gonzalez, "I want to shake your hands." When he'd done that he said, "My family owned a building Leviathan burned down two years ago. The police suspected arson but had no leads. Now they tell me the guy who did it confessed, thanks to you kids. So I want to reward you."

"All right!" Knievel's face lit up. "How much?"

"Pick something. I'll tell you if it's too much."

I knew exactly what I wanted. "Money for camp."

"Me too." Theresa snuggled her face against Pipsqueak. "It's my last chance to be with my best friends before I have to move."

I felt awful. Some friend I'd been!

Mr. Gonzalez looked doubtful. "That sounds expensive."

"Can't that be my reward, too?" Susannah asked. "For Lucy and Theresa to go to camp with me?"

"It's not expensive," said Quiggy. "It's a YWCA camp. But Ruth is paying for you, Theresa. It's her thank-you for saving Pipsqueak." The phone rang and Quiggy went to answer it.

Theresa looked surprised. "Then give my reward to Lucy, so she can go to camp, too."

Now I really felt bad. "Thanks," I mumbled. "Actually, my father can probably pay for some of it."

"Then I think I can manage the rest." Mr. Gonzalez turned to Theresa. "Choose something else."

"What I *really* want is to stay here. But — " She shrugged. "So clothes, I guess."

"And what about you, Ms. Sherlock?"

"Well" — Susannah hesitated — "there *is* one thing I want that my grandparents won't buy for me."

I had an awful feeling I knew what was coming.

"It really is unfair of them." I tried to sound sympathetic. "Who'd mind having a boa constrictor around?"

Susannah beamed at me. "Then you'll keep the boa for me?"

As I sat stunned by that development, Quiggy returned, looking excited.

"That was your social worker, Theresa. They've decided to let you stay. The story in the newspaper convinced them you're fine right here."

Theresa ran to Quiggy with the biggest grin I'd ever seen on her face.

Knievel began telling Mr. Gonzalez what he wanted. "Your basic Mongoose doesn't cost all that much," he said persuasively, "and I bet I can find an old one cheap."

"Sounds affordable," Mr. Gonzalez agreed. "But are mongooses *legal* to have as pets in California?"

Knievel sighed.